T0345537

MONSTERS
LIKE US

THE GERMAN LIST

Ulrike Almut Sandig

MONSTERS
LIKE US

Translated by Karen Leeder

LONDON NEW YORK CALCUTTA

This publication has been supported by a grant from the Goethe-Institut India

Seagull Books, 2022

First published in German as *Monster wie wir* by Ulrike Almut Sandig
© Schöffling & Co., Frankfurt am Main, 2020

First published in English translation by Seagull Books, 2022
English translation © Karen Leeder, 2022

ISBN   978 0 8574 2 983 4

British Library Cataloguing-in-Publication Data
A catalogue record for this book is available from the British Library

Typeset at Seagull Books, Calcutta, India
Printed and bound in the USA by Integrated Books International

CONTENTS

MOONSTER

Well, if you really must go, at least look after the car, you said. But isn't this where it all begins, Voitto, exactly here? In the back of beyond, in the East German sticks and at night, where there should really be two people standing looking at the moon. The moon as it orbits around Mother Earth, that bright bluescreen, on which all of us project our ideas—including you and me. I don't mean the where. I mean the how. Doesn't it all start here?

I'm not a moonster, you said. Your accent sounded like pebbles in your mouth, a cool gust of wind, like sex with your tongue, or just like, I'm not inhuman.

When I play, I'm alone with my instrument. Then I don't need you.

Sometimes I think I recognize your tall figure in the darkness of the auditorium. Your untameable hair lit up by the spotlight while I sit screwing up my eyes, as for a terrible moment the unity between me and the instrument dissolves. But instead of your curls, your casual posture, your finger tapping on the armrest, I only recognize silhouettes of unknown people in the backlight, their heads in rows side by side, standing waves in a seascape, while I keep watch for you. Pull yourself together, I hear Grandfather murmur. Of all people. Don't you love me any more? By now the keys are popping up under my flying fingertips so that I must force the gap between myself and the music until we become a single entity again, the piano and I. I don't need you for that at all. It's about whether someone is out there listening as only you do. Ready to blow me into pieces with sheer love. You're not in the audience, of course.

Instead, I discover Viktor. Viktor in the Philharmonie, Viktor in the Gewandhaus, Viktor in the Handel House. No sooner am I back playing at home than there he is. His broad neck, protruding ears, the blonde head shaved out of habit as much as anything and smack bang in the middle of the auditorium, as if he belonged, without ever quite belonging. His muscular legs spread wide in front of him, his hands folded in his lap, nodding to the beat as if he were at a hip-hop concert. If he notices me looking, he lowers his eyes, as if I had caught him out doing something bad. During the final applause he gets up, pushes his way through the crowded rows and leaves the concert hall.

So, if you want to join me, here in this inhospitable piece of land, come on. Even if only in your head which, you always claimed, was equipped with a brain—unlike mine. So, if you are finally going to put that brain of yours into gear now would be the perfect moment, Voitto. Come on! You won't find the Volvo, it's long gone in the darkness of my own thoughts. But you will find me, standing on a mountain ridge.

Okay, it's less of a mountain ridge than the outer edge of a crater. As wide and deserted as if all of this land east of the Elbe would fit in it, or at least a handful of villages. I'm exaggerating, you say? It's not deserted. I'm there. Seen from here, the earth is even bigger and more beautiful than in all those TV documentaries in the whirlwind of my hotel rooms. It fills my whole field of vision. And, like a really good story, it has neither beginning nor end, but swirls through the pitch dark only to arrive, with musical precision, back where it all began. So once more, from the beginning. Come on. *Da capo al fine.*

I
Ruth

1

Once I was floating in my mother's womb. It was cramped and had walls that gave way as I bumped against them, then nudged me back into the twilight of her body. It was reddish in colour, although I didn't see the relevant documents until decades later. From the other side of the abdominal wall I heard noises, doors opening and closing, an iron hatch, a shovel and the scraping of iron on iron, muted creaking and crackling, a rhythmic thunder like the clatter of coal, and the scratching of oven tongs, interrupted by her voice, that seemed to be telling someone something. I didn't really care what my mother was doing out there. She meant nothing to me in the way that mothers always end up meaning nothing to their own children. Perhaps you can only have an attitude about something when it is separate from you. But I was a tiny, featherlight foetus in dark-brown corduroy trousers hunched in my mother's uterus. And at the same time, I was her womb and was wrapped around myself, threaded with fine veins.

I have no inkling how old I was when I had that dream. In any case, I was not surprised that my brother was there too. We were having fun, laughing and jostling each other as we flew through the darkness like two cosmonauts in a space capsule after a power failure. His head with its protruding ears stood out black against the reddish walls. It didn't surprise me in the slightest that suddenly a crack of daylight burst in and he said, Catch you later, Dummy-doll, I'm going out into the world now. Of course, I wanted to go too and rowed up behind him with my see-through arms, but Fly turned round again; That's not how it works, he said, your turn comes much later. So, I sat cross-legged on the smooth uterine tissue and watched him crawl out through the gap that closed behind him again, and said to myself, That's a shame, but never mind. I'm younger, after all.

I must have been quite small. Because when Fly and I were having a snack in the kitchen and I told him I could remember his birth, he laughed and said that was rubbish, I was four years younger than him. Exactly, I said, scraping my vanilla ice cream out of the beaker. That's why I stayed inside. You said it wasn't my turn yet, don't you remember any more? My brother got up from the kitchen table, snatched hold of a thick black fly for one of his experiments and, keeping it in the hollow cavity between his hands, carried on laughing and explained: Hey, Dummy-doll, we were both in Mummy's tummy, but not both at the same time.

Or does it begin in the midst of it all, in our families, where we get up and go to sleep alongside the others, as if it were self-evident to live just like this and no differently?

In our house no one was beaten. In this, Fly and I were different from most of the children we knew. When the children were together at family gatherings, in the stairwell in search of daddy longlegs (his idea), in the attic in search of the Advent Santa Claus mask from RE classes (my idea), or by the gooseberry bushes in the garden (our cousin from Bitterfeld's idea), while our parents were still sitting in the dining room eating cake, my brother would ask everyone who among us was beaten at home. Which of you get a thrashing? When the daughters of our father's old student friend reported getting clipped round the ear at the dinner table, or our cousin from Bitterfeld hesitantly described the belt that hung behind her mother's mirror, a look of quiet satisfaction passed across my brother's face. Probably I was the only one to see it. Sometimes I pushed past him and said, No, no one ever gets beaten here. Smacked, at most. Where? the student friend's daughters wanted to know. On the bum, of course, I said unmoved and ignored my brother's fist poking me in the ribs. When the Bitterfeld cousin asked: With or without clothes? and before Fly could interrupt, I quickly said: Without, of course, otherwise you don't get the proper smacking sound, I saw the same satisfaction I had recognized on my brother's face flick across my cousin's. She's only saying that so she's the centre of attention, he said, then clipped the back of my head with his hand and ran up the stairs to the attic. Do you want to see a real urn? One with someone in? The daughters of the student friend declined, they also had urns in their attic at home, but the Bitterfeld cousin rushed after him asking: What is an urn? There are dead people's ashes inside, my brother whispered in her ear. When you shake it the tooth crowns rattle, and some of them are made of gold!

That wasn't a real hiding. A hiding is when you can see something afterwards, my brother said.

I'm dying, I'm dying. We were lying in our beds, the headlights of passing cars moving across the bedroom walls. That's not true, I said. You don't die of a hiding.

No, I'm dying of something else, came the voice from his bed. My brother lay on his back wheezing loudly. Can't you see I'm dying? he said, grabbing his neck with both hands, before grunting unintelligibly and throwing himself back and forth on his mattress in spasms. I jumped out of bed and whispered, I'll get Mother. No, no, my brother wheezed, half-suffocating, don't get her. Get me a sweet. A sweet! He grunted pitifully and jerked his face round towards me, ghostly in the darkness.

Are you sure that'll help? I asked, and Fly replied: If you don't go right away, I'll really die, oh, oh . . . I couldn't let that happen. I ran into the kitchen, dragged a chair over in front of the kitchen cupboard, climbed on top and from there on to the shelf, where I fished out a sweet for Fly from the top section and one for me, for reassurance.

What are you up to? I heard a voice behind me. It was Pap. I'm just get something for Fly so he doesn't die, I answered in my defence. The next moment I was lying in bed on my stomach, face pressed into the pillow, and Pap was standing next to me. He pulled the cover back, pulled down my pyjamas and smacked my bottom. Not with any force, but with precision. As if he were banging the side of a broken vending machine, or as if he were himself a machine performing the one and only function for which it has been designed.

But in that case without any in-built language program, as Pap always administered the blows to our backsides in silence. After performing his educational duty, he pulled up our pyjama bottoms, just like that, and tucked the blanket up to our chins. The next morning, the imprint of his hand on our backsides would be long gone.

When Pap closed the bedroom door behind him, I stayed lying on my bed, still on my stomach, crying quietly to myself. It wasn't until I heard my brother's breathing come deep and regular that I stretched out my legs into the cool bottom half of my bed. The headlights of a passing car moved across the ceiling of the room, and I closed my eyes.

Fly and I shared the children's bedroom which had patterned wallpaper and high windows. The headlights of the few cars that turned at the crossing in front of the house moved across the walls, in a window-shape, while I lay in bed with a torch leafing through my mother's songbooks. Many of them were ones we sang in the children's services, I recognized them by the pictures. With my index finger I traced the sounds as they went up and down on the telegraph wires of the stave and pictured them to myself as swallows, landing, singing and rising again. It was quiet in the room; from next door came the monotonous drone of the TV, muffled conversations. But in my head there was a humming, clapping and singing, which, when I looked up from the notes, followed the shining square of light across the walls. When Fly was sent to bed, I quickly turned the torch off and pretended to be asleep.

Don't bother, he said, I've already seen.

I yawned demonstratively and blinked. You woke me up, I murmured convincingly. Hmm, whatever, hissed Fly and pushed a chair over in front of the cupboard. In his pyjamas, he climbed from the chair to the dresser, balanced on the top of the toy cupboard, shouted: My name is Spiderman and leapt into the bed next to mine with a thud.

Fly loved to be in the air. During the day he would take to jumping from the garage roof. Or from the tops of the tall apple trees. Or he climbed up onto the neighbour's pigsty and charged up and down until the piglets began to squeak and my mother ordered him down and sent him to the nursery for cello practice. But Fly found pretty much everything more exciting than cello.

Did you know that glue burns? he asked me and pulled a silver tube out of his back pocket. I was standing on my bed under the window. With my hands pressed flat on the cool inner pane, I was bouncing up and down, absent-mindedly, watching the Soviet soldier in front of the house, who had been dropped off by a car just as I was coming back from kindergarten. You didn't know that did you, said Fly. My mattress springs squeaked like the piglets in our neighbour's sty; the poplar next to the crossroads turned its leaves in the dry May wind; the crossroads in front of the house rose and fell with my jumping. I'll prove it to you, said Fly. The only one standing still was the soldier. He stood in the middle of the crossing, his dusty black boots side by side on the tarmac, his pale hands pressed to the seams of his uniform trousers, his wide head under a helmet that obscured any facial expression. He stood there squinting along the main street. Are you even looking? asked Fly. The Soviet convoys were always preceded by a solitary car that drove the route hours in advance and dropped a soldier off at each junction, instructing him not to move from the spot until the columns of tanks or trucks came down the road, at which point it was his job to point them in the right direction. This one had already been standing there all afternoon. Whenever a car rattled by, a tractor swung past giving him a narrow berth, or boys on their bikes circled him begging him for a military badge, he pressed his lips together and kept looking straight ahead. Dummy-doll, said Fly. It was only when old Pazia leant over the garden fence to offer him a beer in broken Russian that he lowered his chin and shook his head almost imperceptibly. Wait for it, said Fly. 'E has been stationed here for a long time, old Pazia called across to our mother, who had appeared in our driveway, her shopping net on the handlebars, ready to go and fetch sausages before the shop closed. 'E knows exactly what will happen if 'e don't do what e's told. The May sun carved his shadow into the tarmac at the crossing and Fly shouted: And we're off!

There was a click, and I turned round. Fly was standing right next to my bed, Pap's lighter in one hand, the silver-coloured tube in the other. The glue squeezed from the top in a transparent bubble. Fly clicked the lighter again, a spark. If Pap finds out that you . . . , I muttered. A spark, Fly tried it again, a spark, and there it was, a pretty little flame dancing above the lighter. That's not allowed, I said. Fly: Shut up, Dummy-doll, I'm concentrating. The glue caught immediately. In shock Fly pressed the tube and another stripe of glue spurted out, igniting as it fell to the floor. The lino, spread out in shallow waves under a mess of matchbox cars and colouring pens, immediately caught fire. The next moment, waist-high flames were blazing round my bed. I pressed myself back against the cool windowpane and didn't move a muscle. Fly was hopping from one leg to the other trying to trample down the fire, the flames already licking at the wooden bedpost. As he reached out to grab his school bag and beat down the flames like in his Karl May adventure books, the fire was just inching closer to the tube of glue that had fallen on the floor; then it shot up even higher.

Do something, Ruth, he cried. Do something! To reach the window handle, I had to climb out onto the windowsill. Interior window, exterior window. When I finally had it open, the May air gusted in and I felt the fire flare up behind me. The soldier at the crossing pushed back his helmet. Had I called out or not? Did Fly? He was quick. The next moment he had climbed up the porch and swung a black boot over the windowsill. Quick as a flash he grabbed me and Fly and lifted us onto the roof of the porch. Then he disappeared into the room and closed the window. We saw his shape moving around in the smoke behind the glass; he tugged my blanket off the bed and slapped down the flames with precise movements. You rascals, called old Pazia from across the street. We stood stiffly side by side holding hands.

Pap was still wearing his moped helmet when he appeared in front of the porch. As he entered the house and tore open the door to our room, the smoke billowed out of the now open window as the soldier lifted us back in. His face dusty and wet under the helmet he was still wearing. He had a broad nose and the darkest eyes we could ever imagine, and those dark eyes were laughing at us. His huge, pale hand wiped across his face and he coughed. Pap stared at him. *Spasibo*, he muttered. *Spasibo bol'shoe.* The next moment we heard the tanks.

They were crawling slowly down the main road like prehistoric animals, and the soldier ran off, shouting back another *Chert voz'mi*, the meaning of which we didn't have to guess, as he legged it. He charged down the stairs, chased across our yard and the front garden; the tanks on their chains ploughed along the main road, neighbours appearing in the windows; old Pazia stepped back from the fence as the first tank pushed along in front of us. By the time the soldier arrived at the crossing, the first two tanks had already missed the turn.

It took an hour, Pap told Mother in the kitchen that evening, to steer them back and guide them into the road that led to the barracks. He sat at the dinner table with his legs crossed and lit his pipe. It was a different lighter from the one Fly had nicked from him. Of course. Mother stacked the dirty plates in the sink. And the Russian? she asked. Well, there was no end of trouble, Pap said, puffing so the tobacco crackled and glowed. There was one hell of a beating. He will certainly be disciplined and transferred.

Mother span round. But he saved the children!

Naturally, but he had instructions not to move from the spot. Pap sounded as if once again he had to explain an obvious fact that Mother did not know. She screwed up the dishcloth and turned around. He won't, she said. Tomorrow you're going there with something for his superior. Chocolates, brandy, I don't care what.

Pap remained silent and puffed on his pipe. The smoke spread across the half-cleared dinner table and formed a transparent blanket over Pap's head as he leant back. That won't do any good, he said. They have their own rules.

As Mother marched across the kitchen with long strides and stood towering over him, the blanket of pipe smoke drifted up and formed fine curls in the stuffy kitchen air. You're a coward, Mother said. What kind of pastor does that make you?

We heard the slap all the way from the dining room, where we were tucked up on a makeshift mattress bed, staring in concentration at songbooks (me) and Karl May (Fly) so as not to miss anything. The door was ajar. Fly and I had been quartered there until the nursery floor could be re-laid. The whole flat still smelt of burnt plastic.

That is the first slap in this story, Voitto. No idea whether it was Mother or Pap who delivered it and whether it was Pap or Mother on the receiving end. But after a few times round this planet circling the haematoma of the sun, I can tell you this for one: it all starts with believing a slap can be the natural conclusion to a conversation. Fly and I turned over onto our sides and rolled in under our duvets. Then Fly turned off the light.

2

As a child I was as happy and unhappy, as cherished and lost as anyone can be. What kind of child were you? Ah, it doesn't matter what we were, Voitto. Where are you anyway? On the moon one has less of an overview than one might at first suppose. From here the earth looks huge and beautiful and improbably blue, but almost completely round, the perfect simulation of a documentary on Phoenix Channel. But perhaps I am simply too far away to find you or to be found by you.

On Saturday mornings Pap used to come into our room in his striped pyjamas and lie down with my brother on his bed. They lay on their backs, side by side, Pap with his arms crossed under his head and Fly with his messy crewcut resting on Pap's upper arm. They were looking at the cracks in the ceiling and carrying on a conversation under their breath. I caught very little as I was jumping about on my mattress and Mother was shovelling the morning's cold ashes out of the grate. I cannot ever remember being cold.

There was only one occasion I really was cold: after the skating. From somewhere or other Mother had procured some white ice skates for me; wearing them I felt as if I were standing upright on a knife blade, not like in Fly's worn out ice-hockey boots, where the blades always leant lopsidedly on the ice. I had been standing straight as a dye on the local pond enjoying the upright position, while my mother was chatting with a neighbour. The snow from the night before still hung in the trees on the bank and the older kids from the village were playing ice hockey in the middle of the pond. Laughing and shouting, they passed the puck back and forth between them, every so often helping themselves to beer from a crate in the boot of a Trabi they had driven right out onto the ice. The lid of the boot was propped open and, in spite of the cold, the stink of petrol wafted over to my mother and me— probably there was a couple on the back seat snogging in the warmth of the running engine.

The puck made a noise that came back to mind much later, at the Sydney Opera House, when a clarinettist was playing a tricky solo, one without notes and structured only by the clicking of his keys, creating a sound that cut as dryly through the dark interior walls of his instrument as the puck over the cloudy white ice. To this day, woodwind instruments always come to mind when I think about ice hockey.

When my mother had finished her conversation, she took me by the mitten and finally, finally, it was time. There was quite a crowd. With stiff movements, more running than gliding, I moved along beside her. Steam rose from our mouths. My mother turned and circled around me smoothly, talking to me non-stop. If I didn't want to miss what she was telling me, I had to listen all the time. No, I used to be much better at it, she said, but not at your age. That's not bad, Ruth! But careful, not over there, two girls drowned here last year. Didn't you know that? Concentrate, a pirouette, like that—and then that! When we got back to the edge of the pond, the youngsters had finished their game, the Trabi was just setting off, followed by the laughter of the group that straggled off the ice behind it. When my mother took off my skates, I started to wail. My feet and hands had gone stiff and smarted as if they were really on a knife edge. Mechanically, I trotted after my mother, across the large meadow, the cow bridge, past the football field and down the Straße der Jugend. I was yelping with pain. When we got home she pushed me into the bathroom and filled the sink with lukewarm water. Ow, Ow, you're scalding me, I whimpered as I slipped my hands into the water. It just seems like that, Mother reassured me. It's the difference in temperature. Fly and I were the only ones in the family she spoke to like adults. She spoke to Pap as if she herself were a child. That was how it was with us, Voitto.

The chores associated with heating were divided by age. I fetched wood, my older brother got the coal. Once a year the coal van came and poured a black mountain into our yard, higher, much higher than Fly's protruding ears. It took him three afternoons to shovel the coal into the shed, while my mother kept going up to the window and muttering: He'll never do it, he's way too small. And Pap explained, He's a boy. He'll do it. Ruth, go and get the wood.

The logs were stacked next to the washhouse in a storeroom without any lights. Cobwebs hung in the door frame.

The bigger I got, the lower I had to bend so as not to get them caught in my hair. As I picked up the logs in the darkness, I could hear from outside the sounds of Fly throwing coal into the coal shed. Later, in the evening, he would sit at the supper table with his face smeared with coal dust that only made his eyes shine even more seriously. I wanted to shovel coal too.

In the endless evenings of my childhood, my mother would sit by our beds at bedtime and wrestle with some inner demon. But then she would play us songs on her recorder. Another, one more, my brother and I shouted, and my mother would give a pained smile and say she couldn't play any more. When she was out of the room, I could still feel her soft skin on my forehead and cheeks, and I could still hear the clumsy recorder tune ringing in my ears.

Once I dreamt that my mother had a bald patch like Pap. Bald with a balustrade, Fly would have said, from the song, because of the sparse ring of hair at the back of his head and at the sides, but he did not come into this dream. Our parents looked so similar to one another that I could hardly tell them apart. Mother was sitting in the middle of the nursery with her head lowered while Pap was lecturing her. I watched for a while and thought she was grumpy because Pap was talking so much, which was normally her prerogative. Then I looked at his hands. Pap was standing next to my mother; then he took a chisel and split the edges of her bald patch. She cracked like a coconut at Christmas, and my mother held her skull in her hands, and cried and cried.

But sometimes it would suddenly be summer, from one sleep to the next. Then my brother and I fed the neighbour's chickens with the overripe currants from our back garden. We stood behind the bushes, threw the red pearls through the wire-mesh fence and watched as the chickens greedily pecked at them. After a while, they began to stumble and cluck in slow motion, their long-drawn-out cries had something of the old women in the half-empty church on Sundays who swayed as they worked their way through the hymns. We laughed so much we had to clutch our bellies, in which there were just as many currants as in our neighbour's chickens.

Or Pap made a bonfire among the big apple trees. Their crowns were so high that there was room for a fire, Pap thought. Every so often one of the rectory windows would open, and my mother would lean out and shout: You'll burn the whole garden down! Then Pap would laugh and throw another branch on the fire, while Fly and I squatted next to it and pushed potatoes into the embers. When we took them out later and peeled them, blowing our fingers, the potatoes were either charred or still raw. Sometimes an apple fell into the embers. We fetched that out too. It tasted sweet. Pap stood next to the bonfire, arms crossed above his belly, puffing on his pipe, from which a thin twist of smoke rose, as if there was a second bonfire inside, only smaller.

Or Mother packed us into the car and drove with us to the lake. It was stuffy and unbearably noisy in the Trabi, but she would wind down the windows so her blonde hair fluttered in the wind and sing the old songs with us at the top of our voices. 'What kind of trees are these, where the big elephants go walking without stumbling?' we sang in a round, out of tune, as she thundered hell for leather through the pine forests, from one village to the next. The men in their work suits, on the way to some kind of trade deal or other shenanigans, or just on their way home from the agricultural cooperative, all turned around after her.

At the edge of the lake we ducked under the cordon, which ran across the beach like the tail of some prehistoric animal. Sometimes we also went to the outdoor pool on the opposite shore. But there one wasn't safe from the eddies and currents, when the sand far below started to shift. And anyway, Mother found it too crowded over there.

She wore dark swimsuits that revealed as little of her body as possible. What on earth do I look like, she tutted. Bloated. Like a corpse that's been in the water too long. Ophelia at the lake, it makes you want to weep, children, right? Hopefully no one can see me. When she was in the water, her wet hair shone in the evening light and curled up to her chin. Come on, you can do it, she laughed, holding me under my stomach, while I, head thrown back in panic, paddled around her. Wonderful, Ruth, don't cry, you can do it! Come on, I'll show you the dead man.

Then we'd lie on our backs, perfectly still, face turned up to the late afternoon sky. If you think you can't carry on, she said, just lie still on your back and take a deep breath. That way you can't sink, with so much air in your body.

In the middle of the dredging lake was a small, forested island. When Mother and Fly swam out there, as evening started to fall, they would stop and lie on their backs to catch their breath so that Fly could manage the distance. In the evening, the disused gravel transporter on the beach became a dinosaur, with whom I would have long conversations to fill the time until Fly and Mother returned.

You've been here for a while, haven't you? What's your name, anyway?

—

Naaah, I'm just visiting.

—

From Berlin. West Berlin. Every Sunday I get a Kinder egg surprise.

—

How are things with you? You neither? Oh, you're the one dishing out the beatings. That's what it looks like, anyway.

When they finally reached the island, Fly and Mother waved to me, then got back into the water and started to swim back. Two dark, giggling dots in the evening light that slowly grew bigger.

Every year at midsummer, the flying ants would appear. They crawled out of the dark-green painted skirting boards and did their circuits of the children's room. They were larger than normal ants but never took off, just spread their long, transparent wings. As soon as they appeared Fly and I immediately ran wild. How is it they come back every single year, exclaimed

Mother. Unendurable! She sent us out of the room and started spraying the skirting boards with insecticide, while we ran to Pap and watched an evening film in his study. At the scary bits Pap covered my eyes with his hands, but I peeped between his narrow fingers. Once I saw an old man with bald head and the longest fingers in the world looming over a woman's bed. When he opened his mouth to bite her, his pointed canines lit up in the television image. Pap laughed and said that this was nonsense, of course, there was no such thing. Fly laughed, too, but didn't sound convinced. I wasn't convinced either. But Pap's warm hand in front of my face felt good, so I breathed quite calmly and didn't give anything away. If not giving anything away had been an Olympic sport, I could have represented our Republic.

When the insecticide had dispersed and we were able to return to the children's room two hours later, the night finally lay over the rectory like Pap's hand on my face. The windows were open, outside the crickets were chirruping, the summer smells mixed with the last remnants of the poison. I've got an idea, Fly said. Let's tell each other a story every night and take turns one after the other. It's your turn today.

Not fair, I disagreed, I told you one yesterday.

Yesterday we hadn't started taking turns, Fly said, putting his arm on the edge of my bed. And beginning to tickle. You start.

With legs as fat as yours, you shouldn't wear mini-dresses, Pap said.

My mother didn't stop wearing mini-dresses immediately, but gradually. What she stopped immediately was Pap's morning hug. On her birthday, Mother would cut herself a large bouquet of lilac from the tree in the yard. On Pap's birthday, she gave him a box of Lindt chocolates from the Intershop, because that was the first gift he had ever given her. On every birthday and on special holidays they would embrace as awkwardly as children.

But we are different, Voitto. That much is certain.

3

Or, did it all start much earlier, long before the two of us were in the picture? A good story begins well before the first word, and it doesn't stop either. It just keeps on going, even if we think everything has been said and we have long given up on one another.

Pap had been thrown out of school during those days of panic as they started to build the Wall. There had been trouble before. Once he turned up in a leather jacket like the young Brecht: button-down collar and a pointed cut-away neckline featuring an expensive tie, borrowed from his grandfather's collection. His grandfather was the best-dressed man in the little town, which probably had something to do with the fact that he was not from there. When Leipzig came under shelling again in February 1944, Pap's grandfather was at the main station buying English newspapers. As soon as he could leave the air-raid shelter, he boarded the next train and a few hours later turned up in front of his daughter's large detached house adjacent to the factory, sporting just a cardigan, so unusual for him, and with the firm intention of staying.

His son-in-law had no choice. The next morning, Pap's father telegraphed Berlin to have the delivery lorry that took the new season's toy cars to the Berlin department stores come back via Leipzig. Three days later several crates full of books and rolls of film stood in the hall of the family residence, along with travelling trunks and two large suitcases packed with made-to-measure suits. Pap's grandfather wore long underwear, a tie and a top hat, even in summer. But he still cried. He cried because he had only those belongings he had deposited in the storage room of his cinema, just in case. Everything bombed, everything destroyed, he muttered. I will never forgive them for that. Nazi rabble.

But that was your beloved English, Pap's father laughed.

Only the real Brecht could be permitted to dress like that, came the response from the headmaster's office. Copying, on the other hand, is simply that: a cheap imitation of bourgeois bohemian airs, which have long since been overcome in our Socialist Republic. A long time ago!

Another time a classmate had reported that Pap was not only a member of the Christian youth group but also went to church every, but really every, Sunday, and of his own free will, where he would always sit in the same place in the fifth row. Sometimes accompanied by his grandfather with a walking stick and top hat, sometimes alone. How exactly the classmate knew this in so much detail, was lost in the assiduousness of the report.

It was August. People sweated sometimes on account of the heat, sometimes on account of the speeches on the radio. Two weeks before Walter Ulbricht had given the order to secure the borders of the sector from one day to the next, so that the West Berliners could not continue to steal butter from the democratic Eastern sector of Berlin. In the capital, students were sent off to go from house to house, to convince East Berliners that the Wall had been erected for their own protection and would anyway be torn down again in a few years. The stifling claustrophobia found release in political activism. In Pap's small town, student brigades tore down the western antennae from the houses. The members of the political youth group, the Free German Youth or FDJ, were encouraged to wear their blue shirt every day until the pending peace treaty was finally concluded. Even more pressure was put on students to train as voluntary reserve officers after their secondary school leaving certificate. The boys in Pap's tenth grade were also instructed to give their written consent. Pap had just turned sixteen. He was torn: as a convinced member of the FDJ, he wanted to play his part in the construction of socialism. But as a member of the Christian youth group, he had no time for weapons. You find that paradoxical, Voitto? You're right, it is. This country was a living contradiction. Once it was the chicken leg propping up the house that belonged to the terrible witch Baba Yaga in the fairy tale. Then it became the foot that had gone to sleep in that boot of a country, in which I, much later, would get up in the morning and go to bed in the evening.

Pap's teacher, a former Nazi Stormtrooper had managed to save his skin in a comfortable Party Secretary's post. At the end of September, he convened a class meeting after school. The class sat nervously in rows at their desks in their blue shirts sweating a mixture of schadenfreude, incomprehension and a sick feeling of anticipation. Pap was questioned about his—as the former stormtrooper put it in his flawless officialese—lack of willingness to train as a reserve officer.

Pap: I object to military solutions.

Teacher: Your Christianity may be reactionary, my young friend. But it does not stand in the way of supporting a military defence of our socialist reconstruction. Heavens, even Adenauer has blessed nuclear weapons over there. With his own hands!

Pap: I don't think so.

Teacher: But it said so in our *Neues Deutschand* newspaper.

Pap: That doesn't mean it's true.

Pap had questioned the authority of the liberal socialist press. At the end of the class meeting, his classmates dutifully lifted the chairs onto the tables before rushing home. They had half-heartedly, but unanimously, excluded Pap from the FDJ. The teacher had even demanded that Pap should leave his blue shirt behind there and then. When he stubbornly retorted that he would certainly not cycle through the place in a vest, they had at least supported him in that.

The following day, the school council decided that, with immediate effect, only members of the FDJ would be admitted to the institution. In the first class they were due to have

German, they were studying Sturm und Drang. Pap was sent home before the first bell.

He simply cycled home. In his street everything was quiet, people had withdrawn indoors where they sat in front of the radios and continued to sweat. In the kindergarten next to his parents' toy factory, the windows had been shut against the heat of high summer. Only in the yard were things busy with comings and goings. Pap leant his bike against the gate post. He did not go straight over to the family house but climbed up to the upper floor of the factory building, up to the office, where his mother was in charge of the books.

She was busy with the accounts for the deliveries of wood from the previous year. He stopped in front of her desk. Outside, a consignment of small fire engines from the current catalogue was being unloaded, there had been a big order from Prague. Pap's mother took off her glasses, nodded and remained silent. Pap also nodded, although he didn't have any clue what would happen next. He leant over the desk and kissed his mother on the little dimple in her cheek, then turned around and left the office. He would now take off his FDJ shirt and visit the school secretariat for the second time that day, the textbooks had to go back.

He had to wait by the entrance, until the consignment for Prague was stowed away in the hold and the van was manoeuvred out of the driveway. As he slowly nudged his bike between the loading workers, who were taking a break and standing in the shade of the factory building smoking, and turned towards the villa, his mother caught up with him. She wore an elegant green summer hat and her dimple had a determined cast. Silently, they strolled along side by side. His mother perched her little briefcase on Pap's handlebars and stroked his head, as she had done when he was little. And what now? he blurted out finally.

I shall drive to Dresden to the Church district headquarters, she said, and smiled, crinkling her mouth. That is the place one has to go in such cases.

Less than a week later, Pap was a student at a Church-run boarding school in Moritzburg, 90 kilometres from his hometown. The building housed the small school room and the sleeping accommodation with two beds apiece. Food was eaten in the Deacon's house next door, but there was not much. Butter was rationed to 200 grams a head; strangely only jam and sourdough bread were freely available, as much as one could eat.

The little class consisted of six boys and one girl. All had been dismissed from high school for reasons similar to his. Pap was the youngest. There was no tenth class, he went straight into the eleventh.

Never in his life had he really had to set himself to learning. He missed his mother most. He would lie in bed in the evening with his head buzzing until the breathing of his roommate, an asthmatic boy who spent his free time playing the organ in the chapel of the Deacon's house, finally became regular and deep, then he would turn onto his side and switch on the light. Dear Mama, thought Pap, there's so much I have to write to you. (But he didn't write it down.) Dear Mama, how are things in the factory, have the Christmas deliveries started? Please tell Father that I think about you both all the time.

Scarcely had anyone been thrown out into the world more abruptly. There had been no time for tearful goodbyes, so he did not cry; and later, on other occasions, he did not bother either. During the service he did not sit in the gallery with the other boarding-school students, but in his place in the fifth row, his arms crossed in front of his chest. He did not join in during the hymns, because he couldn't sing in tune, but he listened and thought of nothing, not even home. That was the highlight of his week.

The classes were taught by retired teachers who demanded a lot of the young people; because, although the school was not state-run, and therefore could not issue the normal university entrance certificate, it had a reputation to keep up. They received a basic education in Church history, philosophy of religion, ancient Greek, and Latin in order to prepare them for a role as deacon or to enable them to enter the theological seminary in Leipzig. At the same time, they were given the essential high-school curriculum. Lessons took place four times a week, from Wednesday to Saturday. On Sundays, students who had small change for the train ticket, could go home for Sunday afternoon tea.

On Mondays and Tuesdays, Pap and his class attended vocational training in town. Since they had no official apprenticeship, this was where they were further prepared for socialism. Besides his class, there was a handful of girls from a similar Church establishment in Radebeul, some young people with unusual professions, like the boy with the large-framed milk-bottle glasses, who was being trained as a cooper to take over the family business from his father, or fat Konrad, who wanted to become a glazer. In addition, there was the occasional pregnant girl and one or two prostitutes who shared their cigarettes and sandwiches with the boys from the Church school. The teachers had often been transferred for disciplinary reasons and rattled through their lessons without enthusiasm.

On the first day in the vocational school, the seminary students were given clear instructions on how to behave. Best sit in the back row, said their teacher, nervously fiddling with his Party badge. You can play chess or read. Do what you want. But please don't put your hand up.

So that's how it played out. Pap did his time: learnt to play skat or lay with his head on the school desk because he had been up half the night reading Nietzsche. The Church-school kids knew about their special status and would not take any instruction. Once, they all got together and beat up their history teacher. After that he was always very polite to us, Pap laughed, and folded his arms in front of his chest. Impossible, Mother exclaimed, and to think you boast about it even now!

The following year he was the best in his class. Not much of a feat with such a small class, but it increased his popularity. At some point Pap's life in his parents' factory villa became an old song whose words he had forgotten, un-musical as he was.

Even when he had started studying theology in Leipzig, he would sit every Sunday in his same place in St Peter's Church.

Same routine, different city. Pap listened and thought of nothing. After the final blessing, he strolled down into the local ratskeller, where he would only ever eat beef stroganoff. There too he would sit at his same table and imagine that his grandfather was sitting with him and telling him how he had once seen Marlene Dietrich, alone in a nightclub, before anyone knew who she was: Marlene with the blonde curls and the unfathomable look.

If you have eyes as small as yours, you shouldn't really wear black eyeliner, Pap told Mother. That makes them look even smaller.

4

Our neighbour had married a woman with frizzy red hair. She waved me over and showed me the rabbits in the barn next to her laundry room. When I held out a handful of dandelions, they hopped into the far corner and didn't move again until they thought I was long gone. Sport, free! I said to them, and: At ease. That's what Fly, who knew all the chants from school PE lessons, always said.

Then came September, and the earth closet in our stairwell was replaced with a proper toilet, with a white ceramic basin and a long chain in the cistern at the top. During the construction work, we used the outhouse on the neighbour's farm. The wooden door had a sawn-out heart, through which at least a little light fell in. The sharp stench stung my nose.

The following summer, our neighbour's wife had a baby. It was called Matthias. His blue pushchair stood in the shade next to the rectory wall. When I reached my hand in, Matthias' soft fist closed around my finger and didn't let go.

Another summer, and the neighbours argued so loudly that I said to Fly: It's worse than in our house. They argued even when she was at the front door and he was round the back in the entrance to the barn. Once our neighbour had roared himself hoarse, he would always go over to the chicken coup and scatter some grain. After a few weeks, the hens were so huge that they could only bend with difficulty for the currants I threw over the fence.

I told our neighbour about the incident with the soldier. They have to get what's coming to them every so often, he said. Only last month they had looted a field belonging to the local agricultural cooperative and stolen sugar beet. If you're hungry, you get brazen. By the way, it's not just Russians. There are also Ukrainians and Kazaks, even Mongolians. Ukrainians know what it is to be hungry. That's why they're so brazen. He, too, spoke to me like an adult.

Mother's father didn't talk to me at all. He sat in his armchair next to the valve radio and listened to ultra-short wave. Mostly there was bad reception. I imagined the waves pushing the crackling noise from the speakers out into the air of the room. There was no opportunity for conversation, you had to keep your mouth shut. Nevertheless, Grandfather also treated me like an adult.

If he saw me standing in the doorway, when I had been asked to go and say good morning, he would wave me over to him. When I stood in front of him, he beckoned me closer until he could comfortably stretch out his arm and pull me onto his lap. As he bent forward to reach my neck, I kept my eyes fixed on my knees which dangled in the air over the legs of his suit. I was my own doll who didn't want anything and didn't cry, while my grandfather put his lips on my neck and sucked the blood out of me with rhythmic movements, his huge nose tangled in my hair. When the heavy breathing stopped, I stayed sitting there until he pushed me off his lap and reached for the tissue in his trouser pocket to wipe off the red on his lips.

After that he was my grandfather again, listening to the news in his armchair. His cheeks slightly reddened, as if he had taken a walk in the garden, his eyes closed. But I was still a doll and walked stiffly out of the room. The radio waves rolled through the air of the room and made it difficult to move forward. As soon as I closed the door behind me again, quietly so as not to disturb Grandfather listening to the radio, I forgot the bite.

Fly and I were ill. We lay side by side in our beds and spoke as little as Grandfather. From time to time Fly would reach his arm across to the edge of my bed and ask me to tickle it, but my head hurt. From time to time Mother came in and made us leg compresses. The water from her terry cloths ran ice-cold up my legs.

When my temperature had risen even further, I suddenly felt better. The afternoon light shone brightly through the curtain. Mother brought sweet flour soup and put her cool hand on my forehead. If my head hadn't hurt so much, I would have eaten it.

Fly seemed to be doing better too. He was standing on his mattress and had folded the duvet to make a throne, which he threw himself into with gusto. Later we lay back down and played bed ball. To do this, you had to lie on your back and throw the ball up at the ceiling, where ideally it left pale grey marks. At some point, the ball landed on the thermometer. While Fly ran off to fetch Mother, I jumped out of bed and squatted between the broken bits of glass. The mercury was scattered in silvery pearls on the bedroom floor. As soon as I touched one, it disintegrated into hundreds of tiny little beads.

When Mother came, she screamed and grabbed me. Did you put any of this in your mouth? You must never do anything like that, right? Mouth open!

By evening, the fever fell slightly. All the boisterousness faded away. Fly had got up and was eating supper in the kitchen with Pap and Mother. I was lying in the room and was a doll named Ruth. Our puppets lay on the green toy cupboard. They looked around the room wordlessly, their little heads spinning in circles. Only fat Minna had spotted me and grinned at me with her eyes wide open. She must have noticed that I was one of them and envied my body. She only had a head and a dress. I, on the other hand, had the thickest arms and legs in the world. They were so thick that I couldn't move. If someone touched me now, I would disintegrate into hundreds of tiny arms and legs.

Fly was well again. He was hanging around my bed wanting me to get up. But I still had a headache. And I say to you, little girl, arise! he cried like Jesus at the raising of the dead child. When I still didn't move, he jumped on me, grabbed my wrists and held them down in the pillow so he could rub his knees in my armpits. I was laughing and crying at the same time.

Finally, he bared his teeth so that I saw all the gaps for a second, then he bit my neck.

The screaming left me as hoarse as the neighbour after an argument. Fly had long since quit. He was still sitting on my belly, grinning at me, but looked unsettled. Were you really scared just then? he asked. Man, there's no such thing as vampires. Yes, there are, I cried and couldn't even remember how I knew this for sure.

5

When I went back to kindergarten, there was a new child in the group. The boy was half a head taller than me with white-blonde hair. When he laughed, weird wrinkles formed in his cheeks, which scared some people, because then he looked like a troll.

I wasn't scared. I hung upside down on the climbing frame in the yard and watched him. He stood in the corner next to the swings calling out names. Dirk! Sven! Ronny! When one of the boys he'd called ran over to him, he laughed at them without saying anything else. You're crazy, the boys said, and looked at him uneasily for a moment before turning back to their games. After a while I swung down from the climbing frame and stood next to him. You're trying out the names, right? I said. What's yours?

Hmm, he muttered. I don't know them all. He spoke a bit like the soldiers in the Russian Forest. The boy looked at me and attempted a wrinkled smile. Then he raised two fingers, gave the international peace sign and said: I'm Viktor.

Viktor had just moved here. His father was a non-commissioned officer in the barracks of the People's Army of the Republic (NVA), which stood next to the Soviet barracks. He was in charge of the joint manoeuvres with the troops of the 'Soviet Occupying Forces', as Pap liked to call them, laughing to himself. Fly and I would laugh too, even Mother would join in, because they did not look much like occupiers with their shaved heads.

These manoeuvres took place in the Russian Forest, where, as I had discovered shortly before, there were not many Russians. It wasn't even a forest really. Only the outer edges were densely packed with pines and spruce. The entrances were blocked with fallen trees. People gathering mushrooms, or purloining Christmas trees and anyone who had dealings with the Soviets, simply walked round the barriers. If you go deeper in, they reported, there are lighter areas planted with birch where chanterelles grow. If you go right into the heart of the Russian Forest, the forest comes to an end. You get lost in a heathland, a blossoming steppe of luminous-yellow broom and dark, shimmering heather covering the mounds of bunkers and explosion craters.

Once, much later, you and I really did get lost there. The tall trees all looked the same because we were too busy tossing angry reproaches at each other like pine cones. We didn't know about forests. You didn't because all the trees had been cut down where you came from, you said. I didn't either, because we were forbidden to go into the forest. If only we'd had Fly with us. He was never one to let himself be put off by Keep Out signs. But we weren't that far yet. At that time it was only the Soviets, who were regularly desperate there, not us.

They looked dry, Voitto, dry and pale under their shaved heads. Did you have them where you're from? Sometimes they stole hens from the farms at the edge of the forest or stood by the yard-gate asking for cigarettes. Sometimes they had errands in the village and marched along, three steps behind their superior, when he went to fetch our neighbour. He spoke Russian and accompanied them to the fence-maker when new wire mesh was needed, or to the state agricultural cooperative, when the milking machines had to be serviced. If Fly got wind of that, he would drop anything he was doing and stick to their heels. *Znachki pozhaluysta, please, znachki*, he would intone to the soldiers waiting for their superior by the gate to the yard. They shook their heads, but in the end, they always gave him their badges, which glinted like rare metal in the winter air. There were pictures of spacemen, deer, pigeons and of course Soviet stars, but these were worth less when it came to bartering. Fly already had a whole tobacco tin full of *znachki* and exchanged them for foreign stamps. He had lots from the West, even some from the United States of America, also depicting pigeons and spacemen. Fly's godfather lived in Munich and travelled a lot for business. He sent him letters from all of his trips. Fly steamed the stamps off the letters and dried them on the edge of the sink in the bathroom. The ones from Russia, China and Nazi Germany, however, he traded for *znachki*.

Every morning at seven Viktor's father left the main entrance of one of the new building blocks in the neighbouring town and drove to the barracks. On the way, he would drop Viktor off at the kindergarten. He drove a spanking-new Lada, which was so clean and tidy it looked like a police car. You could just see Viktor's shock of blonde hair in the passenger seat as he swept past us children on the Straße der Jugend. A fine dust of snow swirled behind him like the Snow Queen's sleigh. One morning, the snow had fallen knee-high overnight and the pavements had not yet been cleared. The spanking-new Lada stopped next to me, and I got in. Inside it was even bigger than it looked from outside. Viktor's father smiled at me and said something. I didn't respond, but that seemed to be okay. When he smiled, he had the same wrinkles in his face as Viktor.

Later Pap would scold me: You must never get into a car with a strange man, and especially not the Lada belonging to our Non-Commissioned Officer friend, for crying out loud. Then Pap would ask if he had asked me anything. I said yes, and he wanted to know what exactly. I would say truthfully that I hadn't answered anyway, and Pap would pat me on the back and say: Ah, my wise little Ruth. But I didn't tell him that Viktor's father had looked nice.

Viktor and I did not speak a word to each other during the short drive to the kindergarten. But he looked back at me between the two front seats and beamed.

So, half-Russian, Fly said as he picked me up from kindergarten one time. We were walking along the Straße der Jugend. My homemade lunch bag dangled on Fly's chest, where he had hung it round his neck. When he went to school, he was given a proper leather school bag with two light reflectors on the straps. I had inherited the old lunch bag. It was also made of leather, and my aluminium lunch box fitted inside exactly. Fly still loved it. He is not a Russian, I said. They don't even speak Russian at home.

Viktor was strong, I was skilful. In the morning we would sit at the craft table, where he helped me to soften the rock-hard brown lumps of plasticine. In exchange I would make brown snowmen, brown igloos and tiny brown dwarfs, which he dried out in his pocket. At one point he told me that his mother spoke Ukrainian to him. But that's not so good. It is not forbidden though, he explained, adding that I shouldn't tell anyone about the thing with the Ukrainian. I understood. At home things were also said that we were told not to repeat outside.

In the afternoon we knelt in the corner and played families. Viktor was the father, I the mother, and we would always fetch a baby from the baby group. Then we would argue like mad, just as our parents did, until we either fell about laughing or Viktor suggested that we kiss. I pushed him away and told him that only children were kissed, not fathers.

Viktor and I moved up into the same class. Our classroom had patterned wallpaper, in which there were hidden faces, watching us work. We painted spacemen, houses with pointed red roofs and the emblem of our state. The ears of corn were hard to get right with the brush, if one wasn't careful they kept running into the hammer and compass. At break time we would secretly go up to the teacher's desk and look at what she had written. When the lessons started again, we hurried back to our places. We had no say in who was allowed to sit next to each other. But when we were playing Chinese whispers on the mushroom climbing frame in the playground, Viktor and I were always together.

Instead of passing on the message as best we could, we used to whisper our own special things to each other. That he had a moon globe at home with all the craters marked on. With a cable! That I would be signed up for music school as soon as the piano teacher was finally well again, because I absolutely refused to learn another instrument, over my dead body. That I should come over, tonight there were *varenyky* dumplings with sweet quark filling for tea. That's not possible, I have to be home for dinner. Can't you—just this once? That my mother had promised to knead salt dough with us, and he was invited. Roger, Viktor said, I'll come. Over and out.

6

There were lots of photos of my mother as a child. Her father owned a Contax, it had been the first major purchase after their escape. His wife had grumbled. The little ones don't even have any winter coats and you turn up with a camera! But as he adjusted the focal length, the camera made a dry sound, which made him forget all the goings-on in front of the lens. When he was peering through the viewfinder, his family was closer to him than they had been since they had arrived. On the run there hadn't been so many of them, of course; just the two, a boy and a girl. The children hardly noticed when they were freezing and always seemed to be happy. How they all laughed together when he had *obtained* a litre of milk from the Russians! Simply lifted it out of the van, placed his good cufflinks in the empty spot, and a quick getaway. No one had followed him. Who needs cufflinks! They had laughed together until they cried, all four of them.

They had been on the road for two and a half years. They had spent one winter in the gatekeeper's cottage at the vacated concentration camp Mittelbau-Dora in Thuringia. Ice flowers appeared on the inside of the windowpanes, and when the oldest, three years old, licked the slick of ice on the wallpaper, it sometimes happened that he could not unstick his tongue, and my grandfather had to release it with vodka, got through expensive haggling. Before bed, they raced around with the children so that they got warm before crawling under the blankets. They were so funny, the boy and the girl. But since the escape, there were three more of them. Better to photograph them and enjoy them at a distance, before they grew out of the winter clothes again.

On every birthday and at Christmas he called all five children together to stand on the steps in front of the house— for a group picture. Which wasn't that easy. The little ones pulled faces, the middle one refused to do up the top button of her blouse, and the eldest was here a moment ago! Where was he now? And now she really must get back to the kitchen, came the voice of his wife, the potatoes on the stove would be done. Good Heavens, said my grandfather, a single group picture for Hermann's birthday, that must be possible! Well, piped up the eldest, who suddenly appeared behind him, Uncle Hermann will not be able to see it.

The slap rang out. My grandfather took advantage of his family's shocked silence, rushed to the tripod and pressed the button. Playing guitar and being insolent, yes, the eldest could do that. But respect? He wasn't so sure.

The last photo of his little brother Hermann was taken the day before he moved out to the front. After his infantry training, he had been allowed to go home one more time and his mother, knowing about his imminent departure, had insisted on a trip to the photographer. In the picture, Hermann is wearing his hair in a side parting that has slipped a little because he is too young to sit still—he had just celebrated his eighteenth birthday. The front would make a man of him, his mother had said, as he was taking his leave, her tears soaking his collar until the lad became embarrassed. Soon they would only have the photo, but could they have known that? He looked cocky in the picture, a scamp in field uniform. Nothing could knock him for six.

Dearest boy, my grandfather had written to him. He himself had not been drafted. He was considered indispensable for the running of the steelworks where he held a senior engineering post. Dearest boy, you write to us of the sheer terror in your regiment. Every night your mother has stayed up late praying for your safe return. But believe me, it is also not so easy holding the fort here at home. I finally had to write down a list of names for the unlikely event that schoolboys and old men would also be called on to play their part in the final victory. Yesterday the call-up orders went out. All those on my list. Some of them have no teeth left in their mouths. I didn't tell Mama that I was to blame. Do you still have your capsule? Always carry it on you, just in case the worst comes to the worst.

Oh, those photos cost us dear, my mother said when I was looking at the family pictures in the album. In each of them you saw four children laughing into the camera. One briefly wondered about the obvious extent of their quiet joy until one discovered the fifth child, who was not laughing. Sometimes it was one of them, sometimes another. One of us always bore the brunt of it, Mother said. The big ones claim I was picked on less, because I was so small. But I don't think so, she said and turned over the next cobweb page. Look what fun they had. Thank God these pictures are black and white, you can't see my red cheek.

Some had bite marks on their necks. Others had red cheeks, bottoms or their back was black and blue. Some had both. It's like tooth decay, Mother said in passing. She was carrying a bucket of hot water into the dining room and ripped open the bay windows. When she cleaned the window, she always climbed up on the sill. She balanced the bucket next to her, grabbed the crossbeam of the white painted frame and leaned out into the November air to wipe the outside of the upper-most pane. She wanted to have the windows clean before it froze. Everyone cops it at some point, she muttered, and foam dripped down onto her chest. Of course, she didn't wear a housecoat like her neighbours. She would have liked to have been a bit more like them, she came from the neighbouring village, after all. Maybe sit with one of them and drink one too many liqueurs. But she was too dutiful for that. Instead, she thought things normal that weren't. When other people didn't breastfeed because formula milk was so much better than any mother's milk, she breastfed Fly and me for the same length of time as her parents had been on the run, definitely far too long, everyone agreed. When other children had long since been packed off to nursery, so that their mothers could increase the Gross National Product, my mother would sit in the kitchen with us cutting out coloured sheets of paper, which she had wangled from the leader of the Pioneers, the children's section of the FDJ, to make masks, in which Fly and I flitted like colourful ghosts through the garden. When we made camp in the apple trees and vowed never to come down again, she handed sausages and apple juice up to us, so that at least we didn't starve up there. In the evening she folded her hands around mine, and then she prayed with us. She never asked the dear Lord for anything; instead she told him what life was like in this little, ruined boot of a country, which, she said, he would certainly never understand, it was so absurd. God is not a Party Secretary whose favour you can compete for, she said, squeezing goodnight kisses into the eyeholes of our masks. Sometimes when it was already late and we had been asleep for hours, she would get us up out of bed because there was a hedgehog in the garden and we had never seen one, or because family friends from Holland had arrived and brought a strange sweet potato which was supposed to be from New Zealand originally and was called a kiwi. If we couldn't get up in the morning, because we had spent half the night reading, she did not protest against Pap's suggestion that she should make us a strong black tea; just muttered quietly and asked what it was we had been reading. Her sadness was hidden beneath a constant stream of chatter and the weirdest impressions of the other villagers, which even made Pap laugh. But what sadness?

No one is immune to it. You couldn't wring the sponge out for me, Ruth? I took the cooled sponge from her and plunged it in the steaming water. It happens in every good family! I wrung out the sponge, stood on tiptoes and handed it up to Mother. But not us, Ruth. That's right isn't it, Mother said, and gave the uppermost pane another wipe.

Outside someone called over in greeting: Good morning, Frau Pastor! Don't fall out! Mother laughed and called back.

Pap opened the study door behind us. He wasn't happy that Mother was leaning so far out. The neighbours washed the windows without leaning right out, he said. The neighbours didn't have high windows like hers, because they didn't have to live in an old vicarage dating from God knows when, my mother replied, but if it bothered him so much, he could take over the window-cleaning. I heard Pap's steps creak across the hallway. Mother got back in, folded down the inner top window and rested it on the open lower frame. I took the cold sponge from her again and dipped it into the steaming water.

True, I thought. We are like any other good family.

7

All of a sudden it was the summer holidays, and we had time.
Our friends were at holiday camp in the Giant Mountains or
in Hungary, Viktor too. Only Fly and I were still at home. Our
Church retreat would not begin until the week after.

Impossible, Mother muttered, and pulled the dining-room
curtains to. A Soviet lieutenant in front of our house sweating
in the blazing midday sun. Where the footpath had been only
the day before there were now three soldiers digging a ditch,
while the lieutenant stood idle next to them watching them
work. Their bare torsos bent over their work gleamed in the
midday sun. Working the whole morning, and not a single
break! Those poor men, said Mother to herself, and then
raising her voice towards the study: Who got them to come?

The neighbour, came the answer from Pap. He was sitting
at the desk typing the new church newsletter on his typewriter.
Through the open door we could hear the rattling of the keys
interrupted by the little bell at the line ends and the machine
head pushing back. The new waterpipes had to be laid, he
explained distractedly. The lieutenant will be happy if there is
a chance of earning a bit on the side.

Mother was still looking through the curtain and shaking her head. That's impossible! she cried. Those boys won't see any of the money. Not a penny.

Pap got up from his desk and reached for a cigarette with an irritated gesture. Do you perhaps want, he asked breathing out audibly, to go out and do it yourself? Mother bit her tongue and stormed in the direction of the kitchen, where she began to pull drawers out and rattle with cutlery. She called out to us: And you children, please stay away from the curtains. Don't look out, don't even peep!

Of course, we peeped. Every time the lieutenant looked around idly, Fly pulled my hand away from the curtain. Stay away from the curtains, I said, came Mother's voice from the kitchen as she slammed the fridge door shut.

A quarter of an hour later, we saw her emerge from the entrance to the driveway, carrying a tray of sandwiches, three passionfruit lemonades and a bottle of Radeberger. The lieutenant rocked on the tips of his toes as she stood in front of him and addressed him with her few bits of broken Russian. He took the beer from her tray and gave a curt nod towards the house. My mother remained stock still until the three soldiers in the ditch also raised their heads. And, as if she meant nothing by it, she smiled at the lieutenant, put the tray on the wide gatepost and handed the lemonade down to the soldiers. They didn't look exactly grown up, I thought. They were bound to like lemonade.

The summer was hot and oppressive; it seemed as though it would never end. Fly and I had all the time in the world. We ran back and forth to the window to catch a glimpse of the soldiers. Apart from the fact that Mother had forbidden us from looking at them, there was nothing very special about them. But as it was, we couldn't help but keep looking out, to check how far on they were and whether they wouldn't take a break and wave to us, finally. We would have immediately ripped open the windows and tried out our school Russian on them. When I tried to pull the curtain to one side, to get better view, Fly bent my fingers apart until I let go with a yelp. This time Mother did not shoo us away. She stood behind us and could hardly believe her eyes. No, it can't be. Is it really, she muttered. Does that arsehole really have a riding crop in its hand?

The lieutenant stood with his back to us at the edge of the ditch, which had grown several metres longer since the previous day. In his hands, clamped firmly behind his back, a long, thin stick flicked back and forth as the lieutenant rocked on the tips of his toes. Down in the ditch the bent shiny backs of his charges worked on.

Even as we sat mesmerized by the sight of the switch, we heard a familiar engine noise through the window. Pap was coming home from one of his visits, rattling down the road on his Swallow scooter. As he bent into the driveway, he put two fingers on his helmet and nodded to the lieutenant. He, too, could not have missed the switch flicking back and forth. When he opened the door to the apartment five minutes later, he immediately said: No lemonade today and certainly no beer. Otherwise there'll be trouble.

My mother had laid her hand on our heads, I shook it off. Then she turned around and slammed the apartment door behind her. Fly turned to face me. That's it—she's leaving, he said tonelessly. But we only heard the toilet door slamming in the stairwell.

A week later, our neighbour came over for a beer. He sat at the kitchen table and was just raising a glass to Pap, who sat beside him, legs crossed, and returned the toast in a subdued way. Mother was leaning against the kitchen cupboard with her hands on her hips, as if she wanted to give our neighbour his marching orders on the spot. The community thanks its Soviet friends for laying the new waterpipes, our neighbour laughed.

8

In my never-ending childhood, everything happened at once. Fly beheaded flies and mistreated his cello, I charged about with Viktor and let myself be sucked dry by my grandfather. We laughed, wept, understood nothing and ate ice cream; we understood everything and forgot it again. Unnoticed by us, the neurons in our developing brains started making connections, and we learnt more and more. Our parents were caught up with themselves. The endless days flickered by in front of the windows, summer and winter blurred into one.

Viktor and I were bouncing on the sofa. His parents' living room was as empty as the dining room at home but had a TV in the wall unit that was turned off and showed our reflections as we jumped. The sofa had a velvety crimson cover and cushions with deer on, that now lay scattered on the floor. The deer stared impassively up at the ceiling. Viktor clung onto the handle of the window as he bounced and looked out at the telegraph poles in the fields. The new build where he lived was one of the best in the village. The stairwell had recently been renovated and had bright red handrails on the bannisters; central heating hummed in all apartments. Fields stretched away behind the house. In winter deer peered out of the fog, in summer the maize shot up and hid them. We too had gone shouting and laughing into the dark of the greenery and reappeared with armfuls of corn cobs. The unripe ones were white and sweet, we ate them immediately. The ripe ones we took up to Viktor's apartment, stripped off the leaves and boiled them until they sat golden yellow and salty in our hands.

Now the pale winter sun shone through the windows and disappeared in Viktor's rough blonde hair. I jumped around him, giggling, but I could never jump as high as him. At a certain point we couldn't carry on and collapsed on the sofa; me like a sack of flour, Viktor like an athlete after an Olympic victory. I giggled and laughed because he punched his fist in the air like the Black Panthers on the winners' podium.

Pap had told Fly and me about the black athletes in America and had re-enacted their protest with us. Fly and I as Black Panthers at the 1968 Olympics in Mexico City. Me as Tommie Smith, standing on the unmade bed, fist raised; next to me Fly as John Carlos. We each took one of Pap's black leather gloves and raised a child's fist in the air, while Pap stood next to us as Peter Norman stumbling his way through the American national anthem, which we bawled along with enthusiastically. In his theology studies Pap had learnt ancient Greek and Hebrew and before that had suffered Russian lessons for years. But he couldn't speak English any more than his boisterous children. So he cobbled together the American anthem as he understood it: *Odyssey, canoe sea / by the dance leg alight / what's a bubble we held / deadest eggs softly teeming*

. . . We didn't understand a thing and sang our own version. That two people who were truly afraid had nonetheless protested at the way they and their people were treated, while we were still a twinkle in our father's eye, that we understood. I was laughing myself silly at Viktor's raised fist when he suddenly reached out his index finger and pointed at the wall unit. You'll never believe what my brother-in-law does in there.

In the cupboards?

No, in the room behind.

What is, I panted, still out of breath, a brother-in-law, anyway?

The husband of my half-sister, Viktor said. You won't believe what he does to me in there.

I got up again to carry on bouncing, but I was curious and wanted to know. What does he do to you?

He gets me naked.

Huuuh, why? I asked, barely listening.

To bite me.

I turned towards the wall unit and jumped into the air. It's just a bit of fun, Viktor said. I'm supposed to lick his belly. The wall unit jumped up and down in front of my eyes, up and down.

And I lick other parts of his body too, Viktor said.

The lamp also jumped. The door where someone could come in any moment, the whole room jumped.

And then I suck him, Viktor said. Until I get dizzy. He sat stubbornly on the sofa, his body bouncing up and down as I jumped. And my parents sit here and watch TV while I drink him dry, he said. Do you want to see how to do it?

No, I said and jumped as high as I could, as if there really was an Olympics to win. Nothing like that would ever happen to me, I decided.

9

Viktor's father had been married before. His first wife came from Zittau, where he had been enrolled at the military academy. By the time they realized that they didn't really have much to say to one another, they already had a daughter with steel-blue eyes and frizzy dark-brown hair. She was fifteen years older than Viktor, adored her father, as only a child of divorcees can, and had married early, just like him. Her husband had a smile like Paul McCartney. A lovely couple, people in Viktor's block said when they were visiting. When the parents sat in the living room with their daughter of an evening, Viktor's brother-in-law occasionally got up and went to see what Viktor was up too. It sometimes took a while.

If you don't talk about it, then it hasn't really happened. That's right, isn't it, Voitto? That's how we learnt it. Viktor never talked about it again, and I never asked. Even later, when we worked our way through all the vampire movies we could get hold of. There were some things that never happened.

For example, that his big sister and her husband sometimes took care of him. At first only for an odd evening now and then, when Viktor's parents went to a celebration at the local combine, or to the Christmas party at the barracks. Then they played board games in the living room and drank something they called a 'Green meadow', a concoction of orange juice and blue curacao that they had dug up somewhere. It wasn't really a proper game, as Viktor soon realized. The three of them lay around on the dark-red sofa letting him win round after round, while his sister plied him with lots of questions. But they weren't real questions either. What's it like living with your darling Dad? Does he really like his little darling? And your ma, the Matryoshka, does she speak Russian with you? What, no Russian? Can you do French? You don't even know what that is, ha ha! Viktor immersed himself in the game and drank his glass in a single gulp, while his sister and her husband bent double with laughter, pouring him a glass of egg liqueur. Nice and sweet, he likes it sweet, doesn't he? She was still laughing as Viktor ran to the bathroom to be sick.

Her husband then went after him to take care of him. He crouched next to the toilet and pulled Viktor's hair out of his face while he threw up. Your sister didn't have it as easy as you, he said. But you are a good lad and you get it. Viktor hardly registered as his brother-in-law undressed him and put him to bed. His parents were always relieved that their son was sound asleep when they came home late.

The whole thing worked so well that Viktor's older sister and her husband soon stayed over at weekends, when his parents went on company trips or to the Spreewald to have a bit of time for themselves, as they called it. Each time they went away, Viktor's mother took his face into her soft hands and told him not to be naughty. Make sure you do what the grown-ups tell you! Viktor nodded and disappeared into his room; it was filled with the pale glow of the lunar globe.

On such weekends, it was easy for Viktor to do what his sister said. I'm not your nanny, she used to say, standing in front of the wall unit, index finger on the button, looking for the Western stations. You just had to sit next to her watching TV, then you were left alone. Viktor would have liked to have watched TV from morning to night.

But his brother-in-law took to walking through the streets of the new block with him; he was soon as well known as if he really lived with them. They sat on the steps in front of the ice-cream parlour, licking their ice creams, and Viktor had to tell him about himself. Whether he already had a girlfriend. Yes, he did. Whether he'd ever kissed her. No, he hadn't. Whether he would like to. Noooo, not really. Whether he liked the ice cream. Yes, of course! Whether he should teach him how to kiss properly. No. Does he not know when he's having his leg pulled?

In the evening Viktor's brother-in-law lay down with him in bed, pushed up his pyjamas and put his big mouth on Viktor's belly. Kissing works the same as when you lick an ice cream, Viktor. You should be happy that I'm teaching you. You won't learn anything like this from your father. Viktor's sister stood in the bathroom doing her make-up.

Later, when Victor's belly and then his whole body no longer felt that they belonged to him any longer, his brother-in-law stood up and pulled his trousers up. Viktor had closed his eyes and pretended to be asleep. His brother-in-law and sister soon left the flat and went to the disco. They locked the door from outside, and Viktor was a little more alone. Then he rolled onto his side, pulled his legs up and looked at the dark patches of the moon's frozen lava seas.

10

In the mornings his sister and brother-in-law would be sleeping off the night before. A few times Viktor sneaked into the kitchen to get himself a slice of bread and honey. If he got caught, his sister just stayed in bed and called flatly: Don't you let your parents get any sleep either? Until his brother-in-law grabbed him by the collar of his pyjamas and shoved him back into his room. Or Viktor crept to the phone. Maybe to call Matusja and Daddy, although he did not know where to reach them. Or maybe just anybody, by dialling random numbers, until he heard the ring tone, and someone picked up and asked about the snuffling at the other end of the line: But who is there? Say something. Oh, little rascal. When his sister cottoned on, she got angry. From then on, the door to Viktor's room was locked in the mornings.

Then Viktor would stay in bed, roll onto his stomach and grab a book. This is bearable, he thought to himself, finally a bit of peace. If he didn't need to pee too badly, he sometimes managed to fall back to sleep again. But often he needed to go to the toilet so badly that he got dressed and stood by the wall to the bedroom knocking for them to open the damn door. Once they lost their nerve and opened up, but mostly they just didn't seem to hear him. Dear Matusiju, Viktor said to himself. Don't worry, I'm listening carefully. I'm doing what the grown-ups say. I've just wet myself. But did the grown-ups listen to him? Dear God, Viktor prayed, can you hear me? Please make the door open. Sometimes God did him a favour, and the key turned in the lock at the very moment he had been pleading fervently for it to happen.

Once Viktor had to go to the toilet so badly that he finally fished his bread tin out of his school bag. He shat next to the remains of Friday's school lunch and cried as quietly as possible. Outside the children in the neighbourhood had long since been called in for lunch when his door was opened. What's that smell in here, asked his sister wearing the quilted bathrobe belonging to Viktor's mother.

If you don't talk about it, it didn't happen. Viktor did not tell his parents about it when they stood in the hallway on the Sunday evening after an infinitely long weekend, with cheeks red with the fresh air and presents in their hands, a Kinder egg from the Intershop for Viktor and a bar of chocolate for his big sister. Viktor then turned on the heel and disappeared into his room. Would his brother-in-law say anything about what Viktor had let him do? How he had sucked Viktor until he felt as if he could never, ever open his eyes again and look someone in the face? How he then demanded that Viktor suck him too? How he hadn't been able to breathe and thought he would suffocate? And how proud he was when his brother-in-law later punched his arm and said that he really was okay and that Viktor could count on him if ever he was in trouble? Had his sister noticed; perhaps she was angry? Would she tell? Dear God, prayed Viktor, please make it so no one knows. God also did him this favour.

Was everything okay? he heard his father say in the hallway. Gets up nice and early, my sweet little brother, his sister joked. Viktor couldn't catch the rest, standing directly behind the closed door of the bedroom. On the other side, his mother stood with her ear pressed to the door. Don't be so clingy, Dad said. He'll come out when he's ready.

11

When at school the class was asked to write about what our parents did, I wrote my mother is a ca–te–chist and an apo–the–ca–ry. That's not quite right, my mother pointed out. I am just an assistant; the apothecary is my boss. The apothecary was an old man almost the same age as Grandfather; in his white coat and with his long, dyed-black hair, he looked like our local village Einstein. The chemists' shop was a labyrinth of back rooms with back rooms off the back rooms and dark shelves that reached up to the ceiling. Sometimes Pap, Fly and I would pick Mother up there. I would squeeze past the queue, lift the flap in the counter and enter another world.

In this world there were women sitting, running about and standing deep in animated conversation. Like the chemist they all wore white coats, but unlike him they were young and beautiful. They greeted me exuberantly. Goodness, how big I was; did I remember her? asked one. Talking quietly or laughing, they busied themselves sorting out little packets, filling in forms, or sat at workbenches, filling powders into clean moulds, rolling pills, stirring ointments, or measuring out tinctures. One of them, the most beautiful, ran over to me, arms out wide. My Ruth!

I still hadn't started at school when I asked my mother whether she had a cream against vampires. Vampires? she asked, confused. Did Fly tell you about them or was it Pap? There are no such things as vampires. There are, I insisted and showed her my neck. She inspected my neck carefully, for a long time. Her cool rough hands turned my head this way and that so she could see the red marks that Grandfather must have left on my neck. I let it happen, though normally I hated being touched. When she was done, she kissed my neck and confirmed: It's true, there are two nasty horsefly stings. Do they hurt? Odd, just before winter. But hold on a moment—I think I do have a cream for that. And with that she disappeared.

But mostly Mother came home by bus. If there was nothing to get in the way, a Pioneer meeting or Fly, I would go out to the bus stop and wait for her. She stepped down from the light-blue regional bus and smiled down at me with a tired expression. It's good you were there, she said, otherwise I would have just sailed on past.

But sometimes Fly did get in the way. With his free hand he pushed the red sugar bowl across the table. Look, here's the bus passing the church, now it's turning the corner, here is the bus stop. With the other hand he held on to my wrist and slid the salt pot across the table. This is Mother. Look. Now she has got out and is setting off. Hey, look properly. I can tell you exactly when she will unlock the door downstairs. I was grizzling for him to let me go. Now she's passing the Schumanns' house, now Thomas Willi's, now where the Kohls live, this fork is the entrance to our yard. Now she's turning in, crossing the yard to the laundry room at the back, in a minute you'll hear the door. At that moment the back door opened. I cried and wrenched myself free.

And why isn't ca–te–chist right? I wanted to know. Because I have never been trained, said Mother. But you do it so well, I argued, and my mother said nothing for once and smiled.

Almost all the children in my class went to Sunday school— all except Viktor. They only want to go because your mother is the teacher, he said. I raised my eyebrows and nodded in a disparaging way. But I want to go because I believe, he added. He was sitting on our swing in the back part of the garden, the poles were only loosely fixed into the ground and they jumped as we swung. I was standing over Viktor, my feet squeezed to the left and right of his bottom. You believe in God? I asked, looking up at the rusty bar above me, where the chains of the swing grated. Next door our neighbour was yelling at his wife. In a cloudless sky above us we could see the pale afternoon moon swinging. No, I believe in your mother, said Viktor, and quickly added, of course, in God.

Viktor believed in God as much as he believed in my mother. With the smell of the chemist's still on her skin she would sit at the kitchen table, showing us how to make think plaits and candle holders out of salt dough. Fly made artistic reliefs depicting scenes from *The Jungle Book*, finely detailed miniatures with Raksha and the other wolf cubs, including Mowgli—a salty coil of dough with arms and legs and a tiny face. If one of his scenes didn't seem up to scratch, Fly destroyed it again. Fly, why don't you leave me one at least? asked Mother. Don't be so hard on yourself. Viktor followed her instructions to the letter: forming one coil pot after the next and licking his salty fingers in-between. I sat next to him imagining flying dogs, princesses with beards and exact replicas of the moon with all the craters and everything. I gave the moons to Viktor. Now let's do some singing shall we, Ruth. What kinds of trees must there be where the elephants go for a walk without bumping their heads?

Once Viktor made a little cross and unlike his other botched creations, this was perfect. It was the size of this thumb, perfectly smooth and had a little hole that Viktor had made with a cocktail stick. He set it in Mother's open hand. When she had pushed a thread through and went to hang it round his neck, he shook his head and pushed it back towards her. He's not allowed to wear something like that at home, Fly scoffed. So what, he replied and beamed with all his dimples. I made it for your mother, anyhow. She knotted the thread behind her neck and wore the cross for that whole endless winter without it breaking.

12

It was simply a fact of life, Voitto. During the endless years of my childhood our parents would always argue. In summer they argued with the windows closed so that the neighbours wouldn't hear; though at least one of the neighbours argued even more with his beautiful curly-headed wife than Pap did with Mother. Although Pap did not so much argue as explain things in a loud voice that Mother seemed not to have understood—while she did not so much argue as complain, cry and ask for things that Fly and I understood nothing of.

It was no wonder we didn't understand. We did everything in our power not to hear. Fly would clamber up onto the roof and sit with his legs dangling over the edge reading Karl May, or he did experiments with the insects that had the misfortune to end up in his hand. He would pull off their legs or wrap threads round their chitin necks and make them run round in circles until the loud buzzing blotted out the sound of our parents' voices. But that only worked in summer. In winter he broke icicles off the garage and threw them high into the air until they shattered on the branches of the bare apple trees. Then he got on his bike and disappeared to a friend's house for the rest of the afternoon to charge round with his air rifle. As he tore along the street with its black surface, the grit crunched under his wheels.

I also tried not to hear. I would sit in the dining room listening to music. The record player stood on top of the dresser next to a round dumbwaiter that was completely covered in pot plants. They exuded a strange smell of damp earth and mould, while the record player filled the room with music along with a chorus of its crackles and hissing. Once I had placed the diamond stylus in the groove, there was no stopping me. Full volume. I listened to records by the folk singer Gerhard Schöne from start to finish and over again.

My mother noticed and took Fly and me to one of his concerts, that was actually meant for adults. It took place in a packed church in the local town. We weren't the only children. Everywhere there were piles of anoraks and caps. Someone was always bursting into tears or laughing hysterically. We had managed to get seats up in the gallery. All the lights were bright and festive. I was in high spirits. Suddenly darkness fell. I slipped off my seat so I could peer over the balustrade. Gerhard Schöne entered the presbytery, gave a shy glance at the audience and then picked up his guitar. He was wearing a brown woolly jumper. His soft hair tumbled over his shoulders like a girl's. From my seat above him and just to the side I could see the bald spot on the back of his head. I stood on tiptoes for the whole concert so that he would see me—if only he looked up. At the end I was left disappointed. He had looked up once but hadn't batted an eyelid! Somehow I had imagined that he would recognize me. I had spent so many hours listening to his music. But he took no notice of me.

On the record player he recognized me and sang only for me. And I played for him. Soon I knew all the tunes and could accompany him on my violin. If I had had enough I put a Beatles single on for a change. On the sleeve was a picture of a pram with the faces of Ringo, Paul, John and George peering out. I had no idea what they were singing about but it must have been for children. Soon I could play along to their songs too. I played and played until the calluses on my fingertips had painful notches. I kept playing until my parents fell silent in the kitchen and Pap marched determinedly across the hallway to hide in his study. Once I couldn't wait for it to stop and ran into the kitchen and intervened: Can't you just stop?

Mother, *piano*: Ruth, we're not even arguing.

Pap, *mezzo forte*: No?! What's going on then?

Mother, *crescendo*: It's just that we don't quite agree.

Pap, *crescendo*: That's for sure.

Mother, *forte*: And please go and turn down the record player.

Pap, *fortissimo*: This minute. This din is unbearable!

Underneath our apartment was the community room. Services took place there when frost had rendered the church unusable. Inside there was room for twenty-five chairs and an out-of-tune harmonium. Pap also gave confirmation classes in the community room. He patted his charges on the shoulder, in a friendly way, called them all Seppel, whether boys or girls, and gave them the basic knowledge they needed for their confirmation, plus a bit extra. He was especially respected for the bit extra, which consisted of answering any question the young people had that they were not allowed to ask at school. But he was also respected for rapping youngsters on the side of the head with his knuckles; one boy was even said to have flown off his chair. That you go around boasting about it, on top of everything, Mother was outraged. It would just take one person to report that to the high-ups, and that would be that. Pap laughed shamefacedly, but he didn't concede that my mother was right. He fled into his study under cover of the dense cloud of tobacco smoke and disappeared.

I also disappeared. If the community room was not being used, it belonged to me. And above all, the harmonium belonged to me; it stood there in the corner, slightly lopsided and totally wonderful. My legs were too short to be able to reach the pedals from the stool. So I took turns in jumping down to pump air into the pipes and then bobbing back up to press the keys. When Viktor was there, he crouched underneath, while I perched above and tried out notes that went together with my two index fingers. The harmonium wheezed asthmatically. I was proud of every chord I found by accident.

And then suddenly an electric organ appeared. It was a gift from the partner diocese in Holland and smaller than the harmonium, my feet easily reached the stubby little pedals. The organ had two manuals, and the keys were warm and smooth to the touch like the cross Viktor had made that hung round my mother's neck, but I only dared touch the front one.

There I widened my span to six fingers, while Viktor sat next to me and worked his way through the menu. He liked *violin* best, I liked *harpsichord*. If I ran out of tunes, Viktor simply pressed the button on the far right, then the contraption would play 'When Will I See You Again', and although we still couldn't speak any English, we sang along as loudly as we could.

So, what instrument do you want to learn next? my mother asked. Fly had been playing the cello for several years. When he was practising in the dining room, he had a dark-green volume of Karl May hidden under the music. You could play along with him, Mother said. Only piano isn't an option, though. Why not? You know. The teacher at the music school is always ill, and there isn't a replacement.

Organ was one of the choices, but the cantor played so horribly that even Pap noticed. So that was out. Or accordion, but at the demonstration class in the music school I had noticed that the children were tied to the chair backs so that they did not fall off when the instrument was hoisted up. Or viola, but I was too slight for that. Cello was out anyway. Fly already did that. So: violin it was.

The music classes took place in the rooms of the special school in the city, where Grandfather also lived. In the morning the thick, later the quick, Pap joked to encourage me. My teacher always had cold hands and had me stroke the bare strings for months before she trusted me with the other sounds. Greedy Dogs Always Eat! My playing sounded dull, I would have liked to have blocked my ears, but I didn't have my hands free. My teacher saw it differently. So I rode my bike to the music school once, then twice, and later three times a week. Individual lessons, theory lessons, string group. On the way there, I cycled quickly past Grandfather's house by the railway tracks, on the way back as well. But before that I got an ice cream. Always, Voitto, always. The woolly lint of my mittens stuck to the wafer.

Viktor could never keep track of when I had my music lessons. The second I had pedalled off, he would ring our front doorbell. If Pap opened the door, he just frowned at the little Russian and sent him away again. If Fly answered, he laughed at Viktor and slammed the door in his face. If my mother came to the door, she asked him in and fetched him an ice cream from the freezer. Viktor scraped the strawberry ice cream out of his beaker while my mother prepared a potato salad for the Advent celebrations of the congregation's youth group.

Do you know how come I can peel potatoes so quickly? Because as a girl I once had a job in the steelworks' canteen. It wasn't really all that long ago. A whole summer, just peeling potatoes! In the end, I was as fast as the old women with their cracked fingertips. Are you done with your ice cream? Come here, then. I'll show you how to peel potatoes.

But by dinner he has to be back home again, the little Russian, Pap said a little less unkindly, when he briefly popped his head round the kitchen door.

13

But you will stay for dinner, won't you, Viktor's mother said
to me, and gave me a tired but honest smile. When she came
home from the textile factory, she stripped off her blouse
straight away and buttoned herself into her housecoat, which
made her look ten years older at a stroke. She spent the rest
of the afternoon in the kitchen, listening to Radio Kiev on a
little black shortwave radio. Viktor called her Matusja so naturally that I started doing so too at some point. She didn't
mind. Viktor's Matusja looked tired even when she wasn't.

Every now and then she called us to her and pressed a cup
of sweet tea into our hands. In the wall unit stood a framed
black-and-white picture of a palace with an infinite number
of onion towers, the domes shining in front of the high
summer clouds. Is that the Kremlin? I once asked her, out of
breath from a pillow-fight with Viktor. Well, something like
that, she said, smiling. It is the monastery of the caves. What
is a cave monastery? I wanted to know. Ah, it is the most
beautiful thing about Kiev, cried Viktor's Matusja and clapped
her plump little hands together. The churches have golden
cupolas, and the walls are snow white and cool. Inside, it

smells like incense, as if it were always Christmas. And you know what, Ruth, there are underground passages with real mummies in them! I liked the way she chuckled so that her horn-rimmed specs slid along her nose and that I thought they would fall onto the kitchen tiles and shatter into a thousand pieces like mercury.

The surface of Viktor's lunar globe was furrowed with craters, solidified lava seas and grooves. My fingertip fitted exactly into the Copernicus Crater. When the globe was switched on, a cool light filled the children's room. It fell on the carpet, the toy cupboard covered with stickers, the window handle with the sports badges, it turned my yellow cardigan green and beamed into Viktor's face, until his wrinkled smile seemed eerie even to me. You see this thick line? The lunar equator, he said more to himself than to me. On the side furthest from the earth it is much thicker than in front.

It was all double Dutch to me. You old mummy! I cried and threw a last embroidered pillow at him.

No, I'm a vampire, he replied, showing me his snow-white teeth. He was the only one whose vampire jokes I found okay.

Mother wondered where Viktor's and my fascination with vampires had come from. She stood in front of the nursery shelf next to the tiled stove looking at my books. It was a harmless collection. At the very bottom the little white spines of the Pioneer series (deadly dull), above them and thumbed almost to breaking point the *Nesthäkchen* novels and *Ronja: The Robber's Daughter*, and right next to it, *From Anton to*

Zygot—the children's encyclopaedia, with more than 1,450 alphabetically arranged entries and over 1,000 colour illustrations. And next to the bed, songbooks and etudes, which I would leaf through in the evening after bedtime. Absolutely nothing about vampires, she muttered. Where on earth did she get all that from? I don't understand. Ruth?

She hadn't noticed that I had been hunched up on the doorstep, listening to her for a long time, my knees wrapped around.

Ruth, come on. Have you ever borrowed a vampire book from the library?

As if there would ever have been such a thing in the library! The library consisted of precisely two cupboards which stood in an otherwise completely empty room. They were in fact old farmer's linen cupboards. Someone had built in extra compartments, and now the books piled up in them like the trousseau of a maiden great-aunt and exuded a musty smell of old paper. One cupboard for grown-ups and one for children. I had been through the latter a long time ago, but no matter how much I read and searched, I had found as little as Mother about vampires. Are there books about vampires, then? I asked.

Of course there are, said Mother, but they are not suitable. And besides there are no such things as vampires.

But, I insisted again. Grandpa is one.

Mother suddenly turned her face to me. Only now did I see her swollen eyelids. Her nose was reddened, her neck blotchy. Had she been crying? Because of me? I pressed my face into her soft belly and wished I hadn't said that. I was just joking, I laughed, embarrassed. I just meant because Grandpa is so old. I wanted Mother to stroke my head. I couldn't stand it when I was touched. Come here, I thought, go away! I know, my big brave girl, she should say. I saw they weren't horse-fly stings. You don't have to go there any more.

But my mother didn't stroke my head and didn't say anything. We stood on the nursery carpet and might have been mistaken for one of those bronze statues in the local town, except that Mother wasn't so much holding me as I was hiding my face in her sweater. Next, I heard Pap come out of the study and walk through the hallway with somewhat hesitant steps. And as if he had finally reached some decision or other, he pulled the apartment door behind him with a jerk. Mother started. I looked up at her. She had turned her head to the side and looked out of the window of the children's room, from where one could see the courtyard entrance. When my father veered into the street on the Swallow and slowly rattled away, her chin jerked. I will never say that again, I decided, looking at her face. I will never say anything again about what Grandpa does to me.

When I went to pick up my Mother from the bus stop the next day, she stood in the bus door and reached her hand out to me. What's the matter, I asked, aren't you getting out?

Mother smiled, her face puffy, and pulled me up onto the bus. Under her seat was a travel bag. I let myself be pulled onto the seat next to her and suddenly panicked. I didn't even have my jacket with me!

And a whole day too late, she put her arm around me, after all, pressed her face into my hair and muttered: We're going to Grandpa's for a few days. Just you and me. Grandpa will be happy.

I only calmed down when we were sitting round the dinner table at Grandfather's. Mother insisted that it was perfectly normal for us to be spending a few days here, after all Grandfather was her Pap when all was said and done! Don't you see how shabby it looks here? she asked me. It can't hurt if we help get things in order a bit. I need my hardworking little Ruth. Don't you want to help me? No more crying, now. We'll make it lovely here, just the three of us.

My grandfather sat ramrod straight at the dining table and spread his bread with his liver sausage. And how do you imagine that working out, he asked, but it didn't sound like a question. I will not tolerate such a thing in my house.

Mother poked at her cucumber salad. What does that mean, you won't tolerate such a thing? She took a little break, then added: Mum would always have taken us in. She knew how wrong a marriage can go.

This is the third slap in my story, Voitto. I will tell you about the others too if you have not found me by then. But we are still sitting in my grandfather's dining room, him pretending I am not in the room. And just like you watch the moon track across the night sky without ever seeing it actually move, Mother's cheek slowly turned red. She stayed as straight as Grandfather and continued to poke her cucumber salad.

Maybe she swayed back and forth a little, maybe it was only I who swayed. When the cuckoo clock that Grandfather had given my grandmother for their silver wedding anniversary began to chime cuckoo cuckoo cuckoo cuckoo cuckoo cuckoo cuckoo cuckoo, and a brightly coloured little man shot out of the door and did his circuit, I finally leapt out of my chair and ran out.

We stayed a few weeks. I thought it would last for ever. Fly is staying with Pap for now, Mother said. You think that's weird? I do too. But someone has to take care of your father. I understood that. When Pap brought me my school things and a backpack with my winter clothes, he smelt of three packs of Czech Camels without filters. Mother hadn't let him in, we were standing in the apartment door. Hey, Pap, I started, folding my arms in front of my chest, as he did, so why do you always argue?

Pap looked to the side and breathed audibly. Steam rose from his mouth and dissipated in the entrance to the house. Then he pressed the violin case into my hand and left. Don't forget to practise, he said on the stairs, then he was gone.

I didn't forget. Instead, I was so caught up in practising that I forgot anything else. In the attic the western antenna perched like a benign giant insect. Along with old wooden skis, boxes, even more boxes, a huge lampshade, and a house phone from Mother's childhood. It was made of black Bakelite and had a dial that I turned so as to listen to the sound of it falling back into place. But unlike Viktor, I never chanced on another connection. At seven it rang, it was

Mother. Oh, there you are, I heard her voice echoing in the earpiece. Come down for tea, there's chicory salad.

Before that, I had time. I played my Ševčík etudes ready for going up into the third grade, then little minuets by Mozart, while the hail rattled against the skylight and the wind reached into the beams. The rosin exuded a smell of resin and concentration. I played the Snow Waltz we were practising in the string group. If I was through with it, I played songs from the records at home. I didn't think about anything, and that was the best thing about it.

Downstairs, the generational cold war crackled. In the morning, Mother fetched coals from the cellar, in the evening she made Grandfather chicory salad with sugar, just as Grandmother had always made it. Hey, Daddy, she said, and handed him another slice of bread, you don't know what's going on at home. He didn't want to know either, said Grandfather, and the sugar crystals crunched between his teeth. One should never leave one's husband. Especially not as a pastor's wife and as a mother. In such moments, he knew exactly how old he was and what to think of life.

On other occasions, he wasn't so sure. Hermann! he called across the courtyard. Mum says you should come in! But Viktor did not want to come in, nor to be called Hermann. I'm not going inside if someone calls me Hermann, he said defensively and tried not to think that my mother was inside, sitting on the sofa and certainly not as tired as his Matusja. Was she still wearing his cross? He will shut me in somewhere, said Viktor, practising throwing sticks, and I'll never be able to get out again!

Nonsense, I disagreed. Why should he shut you in? But he knew what was at stake. Your grandpa has a screw loose, Viktor said.

Better not to tell Viktor that he was also a vampire.

Grandfather, who was still standing by the steps in front of the house, looked unsure. Hermann? he cried, and suddenly sounded like a child on whom someone played a nasty prank. But he had no luck. Viktor shook his head and would not be persuaded.

So, we played outside. The snow lay knee deep under a wafer-thin layer of ice that cracked under our winter boots. We threw ourselves onto our backs and rowed with our arms to make angels in the snow. I'm not exactly an angel, Viktor laughed. We built a snowman with insignia made of crown corks on his thick shoulders and laughed because he looked exactly like Viktor's father. And when it snowed again over-night, and the snow was waist deep, we carved out blocks and poured water over them, so that they could be frozen and made into ice. Twelve pieces were needed to build an igloo. Then we could move in and live in it for the winter. Ruth and Viktor, the last human children to survive, alone among vampires, but well hidden in the perma ice.

At some point, Mother came outside to call me into the house. Dark had already fallen. Our gloves were wet, our faces freezing cold, when Viktor suddenly patted down a snowball and hurled it straight into my mother's face. We held our breaths. My mother stumbled like after Grandfather's slap, her mouth changed shape, forming a huge O, as if she were about to burst out crying. Still laughing, I ran towards her and flung my arms around her belly, as if Viktor had done God knows what. But my mother's O turned into a loud Ooh just you wait! And we pelted one another with snowballs. We ripped off our gloves. We screeched, all three of us, grabbing handfuls of snow and hurling them at each other's heads, we rubbed our faces with snow, laughing and crying at the same time, and as long as we laughed, we forgot all our fears. My mother forgot her fear of leaving; Viktor his brother-in-law; and I my grandfather.

In the end, we were left just crying. Mother scooped the snow out from of our collars and rubbed our stiff hands, and she was probably crying too. But even as we cried, we were still roaring—seized by a silent spasm of laughter that seemed like it would never end.

14

That evening Viktor might almost have come in. I would have kept Grandfather away from him. I would have shown him the attic, the antenna pointed West, the skylight, from which one could see right up to the new quarter where he lived. I would have shown Viktor that the door to the loft was warped and was always open a crack so that it could not be locked. He would have liked that. Up there, in the lightness of wood and air, I would have told him that Grandfather still visited me in the evenings. But only maybe.

Mother's childhood bedroom was at the back of the large apartment. A train line passed right in front of the window. Ding ding, rang the barrier into the silence of the street. The beds had metal frames painted white. Grandfather had bought them from a hospital after the war. Our things lay scattered on one. Mother's fine stockings, tangled with my corduroy trousers, along with schoolbooks, a driver's licence, a post-office savings book, cigarettes. Mother and I slept in the other beds.

In the kitchen and the parlour you couldn't hear anything that went on at the back of the house. As soon as the light was out, we jumped out of our beds and scampered under the covers of our eldest sister's bed, Mother said. We weren't exactly quiet! And as if to demonstrate, she pulled off her slippers and slipped into my bed. It was warm, and we talked for a while until I pushed her away and sleep came over me. I didn't register her slipping out of my bed to go back to the living room, to smoke and turn over in her mind where she could go with Fly and me, if she didn't go back. Outside the freight wagons thundered by and set their rhythms for the night.

Grandfather used to go to bed earlier than Mother. He never did it without looking in on me one more time in my room. He sat next to my bed with his straight back. I kept my eyes tightly shut and pretended to sleep. Ding ding, the barrier rang out and closed before the next freight train thundered by. Eyes fixed on the window, he put his hand under my pyjamas and began to caress me. Or did he? With his back ramrod straight Grandfather sat at my bedside, breathing heavily, and sounding more and more like a very old, crying child. Ding ding, rang the barrier in front of the house. If only I could believe hard enough that I really was asleep, and that Grandfather was nothing but the darkness, thundering outside my body, thundering by and nothing to do with me. With his back ramrod straight, my grandfather groaned and forgot it in the same moment. The trick was to forget it yourself. Ding ding, rang the barrier and reopened. My grandfather got up and wiped the blood from his lips with a handkerchief. The handkerchief still in his hand, he looked around, as if he did not know where he was. When he finally found the door, he turned round and walked out of the room without a word.

I lay there in the darkness, waiting for Mother to tiptoe through Grandfather's bedroom and come into our room and fall into her hospital bed. Then we lay there as if we were sick. And we really were sick, each of us for a different reason.

But that evening too Viktor walked to the garden gate and then to the left, over the tracks and past the station behind which the new building area began. Even later I didn't tell him what Grandfather did. And you too, Voitto, will have to piece it together.

I know what you're thinking right now. Just be clear and unambiguous! But nothing was clear. Did he come to me every night—or was it just once? Was it really Grandfather—or just a bad dream that I dreamt over and over again? There was something not right about this story. So I decided all of it was nonsense. The days were still dark. At school I would fall asleep until Viktor poked me in the ribs because the teacher had asked me something. I was always tired. I slept with my eyes open. Ruth, the teacher asked, and bent down next to my ear. Perhaps you'd like to tell us what you're thinking about? But I wasn't thinking about anything.

Viktor, too, thought of nothing. He excelled in his Russian homework. Not that it was especially easy for him. But he had a reputation to keep up. When he stood in front of the class and talked about the sights of Kiev, Soviet state capital, he would mumble so the teacher would not hear Ukrainian in his Russian. Otherwise, he only stood out in the playground. He acquired a dark-green bomber jacket, the lining of which flashed an invincible orange when he wore it open, and he rolled up his trouser legs. He took to hanging out with older guys who showed him how to build up his biceps and make himself look at least sixteen.

The snow had melted, but it was still the depths of winter. The fields behind Viktor's house lay as if dead under the overcast sky. We were holed up in the bus shelter on the side of the street eating knackwurste pinched from Matusja's fridge. I'm not going back, I said.

Viktor: To your bonkers grandpa?

Me: —

Viktor: Why? Does he call you Hermann too?

Me: —

Viktor: What then?

Me: —

Viktor: —

Me: Whatever. I'm not going back.

Viktor: And what about your mother?

Me: How do you mean?

Viktor: You can't leave her with that idiot.

Me: I'm not going to. We're going home.

We're going home now, I said to my mother, getting my back-pack out from under the hospital bed. Mother stood in the doorway and looked as if she had been crying again. That's not your decision, she said and her chin twitched.

Yes it is, I replied. Why had it taken me so long? I just said, If you can't decide anything, then it is down to me.

Mother looked at me as if I was Pap. Then she drew her hand back and slapped me. That was the fourth slap in the face, Voitto.

Pap and Fly picked us up. Fly in his new parka and with fluff on his upper lip, which I hadn't noticed when we met at school. He took my backpack off and patted me on the back uncertainly. Pap greeted me with an equally uncertain kiss on the forehead and immediately turned to Grandfather. Would he manage okay? They would come by tomorrow and bring him some supplies. Did he still have enough coal? Grandfather nodded to him in a business-like way. When he said goodbye, he suddenly stroked my mother's cheek. Mother raised her eyebrows in surprise and exchanged a look with me. Bye-bye, Mum, Grandfather said to her. See you soon.

When Pap steered the Trabi into the entrance of the courtyard, it was almost as if we were just coming back from a trip away. We peeled ourselves out of the car, asking one another questions and answering all at once: Oh I see, last week, could you fetch, by the way—as if nothing had happened. Everyone did their job. Fly went to fetch coal first. Pap carried Mother's travel bag and my backpack upstairs. Mother withdrew to the kitchen and made coffee. We were a well-rehearsed team going into the next round.

15

Pap took to going over to Grandfather's every morning to make sure his apartment was warm. When Mother came home from the pharmacy in the afternoon, she stayed on the bus and went straight over to Grandfather's, only without a travel bag. She brought him his shopping, cleaned up, exchanged a few words with him and hurried back home to be in time for the evening meal. Grandfather is getting old, she explained to me, but I shrugged my shoulders and rubbed rosin on my violin bow. The fact that Mother and I had lived with Grandfather over the winter seemed to be about his getting older now and not Mother's sadness. Had she ever argued with Pap? What a stupid question, said Fly. Don't tell me you've forgotten that.

When I played violin, I forgot everything. I resumed the habit I'd got into at Grandfather's house and took to playing in the attic. Sometimes there were urns standing about ready for a funeral. Sometimes Mother came and sat down on the dusty-red daybed to listen to me a little. You play as if you had never done anything else, she muttered and shook her head. Why don't you play downstairs with us? I shrugged my shoulders and leafed through my Tchaikovsky. Once Viktor visited. They sat side by side on the daybed and something in my playing made them clasp one another's hands. Everyone seemed to feel something when I was playing. Just not me. But that was fine.

At dinner now, the radio was always on. Pap fiddled endlessly with the buttons, put it on the windowsill, extended the antenna with a fork, cursed the good weather, but the reception for Western broadcasters remained miserable. If the sky was obscured with cloud cover, transmission seemed to work better. Then after the supper things had been cleared away, Pap and Fly would stay behind at the kitchen table for a while discussing the Western news, Pap smoking, with his feet on the table, Fly with lemonade, rocking back and forth on his chair. The wave of refugees fleeing via Hungary had grown to dizzying heights and far beyond anything the old men in the People's Parliament could deal with.

Doesn't old Honni make you feel sorry for him? Pap asked cheerfully as we sat together one evening, he could hardly raise his hand at the autumn parade! Pap raised his flat hand and gave a doddery wave which even Mother laughed at.

My parents didn't even get round to making up. In the evenings Pap jumped into the Trabi and drove over to Grandfather's, as he had a better reception. Together they saw the tear-stained faces of the new arrivals in Bavaria, who said to camera: Who would have believed it would ever come to this? Grandfather sat in the armchair next to him, trembling. Whether it was the excitement about the new era, or the long winter, he had become stick thin. He refused woollen blankets.

With his grey suit and impeccable posture, he sat in front of the TV, shaking his head and explaining to Pap that the final victory was imminent, but now it would be the turn of the boys and old men to be called up.

Viktor got to learn more than me about the precarious balance between violence and the power of state. Rumours were doing the rounds in the army. The heating was gurgling on a cold February evening as his father set down his knife and fork and said: This is not going to last much longer. We must think about what we are going to do.

Matusja looked up from her plate and shook her head. But darling, she cried, this will last to the end of our days!

Viktor's father just shook his head: There was another one shot in Berlin. His name sounds somehow English. People are starting to protest.

But darling, Matusja said again, anyone shooting to miss can make a mistake from time to time!

And Viktor, who felt the enormity of what Matusja was saying and wanted to come to her aid, swallowed down the rest of his bread and repeated as best he could the freshly imparted wisdom from his first year of socialist citizenship classes: They do sometimes shoot at the border, but only in extreme cases, and only after three warnings. That's right, isn't it?

His father looked at him for a long time and said nothing.

Darling, Matusja cried again. But as was the custom in our families, Viktor's father said nothing more.

The sense of tense expectation grew when Matusja watched TV and could hardly believe her eyes. Young priests and laymen with determined faces speaking into crackling microphones on the concrete squares in front of churches from Khmelnytskyi to Kiev. At the very least they said, they were demanding a return of their churches to the Ukrainian Greek Catholic Church, which as a Uniate church was subordinate to the Pope.

My God, Rome, Matusja muttered in Ukrainian. That won't last long either. And it wasn't entirely clear whether she meant the Soviet Union, the Pope, or even God.

Viktor heard everything through the door that stood ajar. When he was not locked in by his brother-in-law or sister, he always left the door open and paid careful attention to make sure it did not close accidentally. He hated nothing more than enclosed spaces. He loved nothing more than big muscles. That was a proper goal, he thought, listening to Matusja's comments on the Soviet broadcaster's newsreels. He lay on the bedroom floor with his stockinged feet jammed under the drawer under his bed. Thirty-one, he said, counting his sit-ups, thirty-two. Viktor was eleven years old and wanted a washboard belly. Thirty-three, thirty-four . . .

Thirty-five? asked Marcel, the Adam's apple at this throat as visible as the butterfly knife in his trouser pocket. They were standing at the bus stop, waiting for the school bus. Marcel was already in the ninth grade, dark beard fluff already visible on his upper lip. He took out the knife and twirled it round a few times with great skill. It was a cold March morning, but he didn't notice how stiff his fingers were. The knife flashed between Viktor and Marcel and reflected the headlights of the school bus as it drew near. Marcel pushed it deliberately slowly into the sleeve of his bomber jacket and breathed his steaming breath into Viktor's face. Only thirty-five?

I can do double that, said Viktor, thinking immediately: I'm an idiot. Marcel exchanged an amused glance with his friends. Well then, do that, little Russian boy, he said. Seventy sit-ups, and you can come with us to the football pitch afterwards. Fewer, and you don't get to come . . . But even before Marcel was finished, Viktor's smile hit him. Dimples played round his mouth that looked like premature wrinkles and gave him an expression of absolute determination, in which Marcel and his friends recognized themselves. This pipsqueak with the diabolical smile was capable, all right. When, despite the suspicious glances of the bus driver, they clambered awkwardly onto the school bus, Viktor already had an appointment for later in the smoking corner.

Of course, he didn't manage the seventy sit-ups. But he was simply one of the gang, whatever. In the evening at the football they pressed his first bottle of Radeberger into his hand. Viktor gulped it down without pulling a face. The early spring light moved in sharply defined cloud formations over the sheds of the agricultural cooperative and the grass as Viktor threw up by the goalpost. The others stood round smirking in a friendly way. Marcel held Viktor by the neck and thought: He's kind of creepy. Goes along with everything and gives that wrinkly smile, as if he had already experienced all sorts.

Viktor thought: Right. Now I'm safe. I'm on the right side.

And he was. Viktor was under Marcel's special care. In the schoolyard, he hung about with him and his gang behind the sports hall. When the bell rang, they went into the school building as a group, shoving the younger kids and the other arseholes aside and separated just before their respective class-rooms. In the afternoon they hung out together at the football field. If the local team were playing, they cheered it on and believed it would win even if they played like shit. When the field was empty, they watched the spring—imperceptibly painting the lawn and trees in delicate shades of green—and didn't mince their words: That at home the gogglebox was practically melting because Gorbachev had signed a decree to reduce the military forces. That the Czechs and Poles had been getting rid of people from the army for weeks. That this was a right dump in the back of beyond and that not even Eastern TV got proper reception, really now! But that they wouldn't leave like the other traitors. That you just have to stick together. Viktor, a head smaller than everyone else, nodded and kept his thoughts to himself. He thought of his brother-in-law and half-sister as little as possible. And before long he also managed seventy sit-ups, with the whole group standing round clapping and whooping.

I hardly got wind of Viktor's new friends. Months had passed since Mother and my time with Grandfather, but I was still in that catatonic state into which vampires put their vic-tims, so that they don't move while being bitten and make everything worse. The vampire's victim never fights back because he is in a hypnotic state, Fly lectured. He feels the pain of the bite, but can't cry out for help. Are you spooked, Dummy-doll?

But why be spooked by something you have already experienced? I didn't even listen. I was a doll with a stack of music books next to my bed. After Fly had been chucked out of music school, because he hadn't met the minimum requirements of the theory course for the third year running and couldn't even transpose from C to E, his cello music now lay next to my bed too. Soon I had figured out how to read the bass key, and no longer had to calculate up from F. If you are not counting any more, you can hear the music properly. And the songs that my brother never played sounded in my ears as Fly lay on his side of the room, which he had separated from mine with our wardrobe, and asked, Dummy-doll, what's that tune you're humming?

Every now and then I would pull Fly's cello out from his corner behind the red daybed. I liked the wide fretboard, the thick strings under my fingertips and the way my hand disappeared from sight when I was playing, and sometimes Pap came up the stairs to the attic to lean against a beam and listen to me. You're playing as if you really could play, he joked. But after Fly had given back the cello at the end of the school year, I didn't miss it anymore and, like an old habit, picked up my violin again. His music books hadn't been on loan so I could keep them.

Soon I could read notes in different keys, as if I were reading stories. I hung the melodies up like tightropes in my head and moved along them, hand over hand, determined not to feel my own fingertips or the rest of my body.

On 8 May, for the first time the People's Police surrounded the participants at a 'Prayer for Peace' service in the Nikolai Church in Leipzig. Pap knew the pastor who had organized it from back in the seminary, a friendly man with brown eyes who wore a leather jacket. From then on, he would drive to Leipzig every Monday. Sometimes he took Fly with him.

While the pastor in the leather jacket read out a protest letter from thirty people to the Chinese Embassy at the end of June to protest against the executions in China, Fly climbed up the facade of the Old Nikolai School so he could see better. Like Zacchaeus in the tree, he observed the growing number of listeners with a mixture of enthusiasm and fear of the police who lurked at the outer edges of the crowd. And then he slipped. The result: two arm fractures and a caution for Pap on account of neglect of parental responsibility and of causing public disturbance, although the 'Prayer for Peace' caused a lot more public disturbance. My brother was probably the only casualty of the whole revolution.

II

Viktor

1

He is standing in front of a coin-operated telephone and his school-French still barely extends beyond *The Little Prince*. He is carrying a backpack emblazoned with the green-and-white logo of the East Elbe District Transport Company. A gift from his father, so he doesn't forget where he comes from—with a crane on his back he will always find his way home. As if he ever wanted to go home again! But only after a year, his father had continued, and given him a friendly clip to the back of his head: he should see something of the world, if only the West.

The sewn-on badge reflects the late-afternoon light behind him. The narrow straps cut into his olive-coloured bomber jacket and make him look even more muscular than he already is. Except for the backpack, he has nothing with him. He is standing in front of a coin-operated phone in the station front hall, twenty-six hours by train from home, he cocks his head to one side, rehearsing what he is going to say in just a moment, in French.

His parents had come with him for part of the journey. He towered over them, a whole head taller, a head that sat on the kind of neck that would be called a bull neck in an adult man. Whether it was the new times, or the years of working out on the bedroom carpet and later in the school gym, in any case he looked gigantic next to them. But growing up takes place from the outside in, which is why, despite his stature, he was no more than an overgrown boy, whose father clips him on the back of his head when he says goodbye.

His father in a tie, the pointed end of which trembled in the evening wind like a compass needle. His mother in her good blouse, with a crocheted handkerchief in her hand. As the train began to move, they raised their arms and burst out laughing—perhaps out of relief that the farewells would finally come to an end, or else to hide the fact that they had already been crying for some time. His mother swayed slightly and waved her arms. His father shouted something at him with the facial expression of someone who had saved up the most important thing for the last moment. But his son only saw his mouth moving and couldn't understand a word. This would happen to him more often from now on. Even before the platform began to move in the compartment window, taking his parents with it, making them smaller and smaller until they were no longer visible, he turned away.

He was in a couchette compartment. His fellow passengers seemed to have been watching him for some time, so absorbed were they in what he was doing. There were two young women with friendship bracelets on their narrow wrists, who were on their way to Belgium to start jobs as waitresses—as they never stopped mentioning. Then a Polish surgeon on his way to North Rhein-Westphalia to do some building work. And finally, a pair of journalists looking for a channel that would broadcast their reports on the long-running reconstruction of former Chechen war sites.

Everyone watched the boy with mixed feelings, as travellers watch someone like him: a hint of mockery about how wet behind the ears he was, a hint of fear on account of his stature, a hint of collective memory. Are Germans today allowed to look quite like that, their hair cropped quite so close . . . ?

As he turned away from the window, the compartment sprang to life. The surgeon jumped up and lifted the backpack onto the luggage rack to prove to the boy, who was a good head taller than him, . . . God knows what. The female journalist pressed hard-boiled eggs on the other women in the carriage and told them about their children who had gone to Paris and found work there, her daughter as an interpreter and her son as a research assistant at an Institute for Slavic Studies. Their children had always had a natural love of languages, she explained, and her travelling companions could doubtless speak French too? Well, the women muttered, while the surgeon placed his hand gently on the boy's shoulder and asked him about his plans in polished German with an accent. The boy reeled off his prepared sentences: where he was from, where he was going, and with that he had already mastered the alpha and omega of all travellers, which dissolves into thin air as soon as one says it. It wouldn't be long before he hardly knew where he came from. Is that right? said the surgeon and didn't know what else to say. The women with the friendship bracelets, who understood very little, nodded politely and went back to gazing out at the villages and pre-fab settlements that lay scattered under the humming telegraph lines in the evening light. This country dragged on for longer than they thought possible, although they came from one that was twice the size that everyone nevertheless thought was a part of Russia, including Russia itself. When the journalist turned off the compartment light so as to be able to get a better view outside, the other women headed off to the train toilet together and came back in pastel-coloured pyjamas whose glitter motifs shimmered in the dark of the compartment as they passed the illuminated parking lots of the wholesale markets. Place after place passed by and sank into the darkness. They passed ribbon developments and portacabins, industrial areas and warehouses, which already looked West German, or were the travellers simply imagining it? On and on sped the train towards Hamm, where they would stop for an hour. The surgeon stood smoking in the corridor leading to the next compartment. When he finally came back in, exuding a smell of cold nicotine, he sighed loudly, but no one heard apart from the boy, as all the others had long since fallen into the anaesthetized slumber of the train passenger. But the boy sat hunched on his seat looking out as the deserted railway stations popped up in the compartment window, passed silently and disappeared again: Braunschweig, Baden-Baden, Constance, then back up to Hanover and Kiel, they seemed to be zigzagging back and forth across Germany, always looking for a platform where the night train might stop for a while without getting in the way of the freight trains hurtling through the night. Three times everyone was woken by border police shining torches in their faces, even though they were in the middle of Germany, or precisely because of it. Each time the boy held his breath even though he had all the right papers, while to those looking at him he seemed completely unperturbed as he stiffly held out his German passport. Looking like he was above it all was a skill that he had perfected years ago, though others around him couldn't have known that. German stations are just as deserted as the Polish ones, thought the surgeon, before falling asleep again. The platforms swam in the yellowish light, as did the deserted station area. It's a funny coincidence, the way this border has been drawn, one always automatically ends up on the wrong side, was his last thought. And then he thought nothing any longer. Between nothing and nothing—the cones of light cast by the endless columns of long-distance lorries from Eastern Europe, trundling along the motorways on their way to the West. The train in which the boy sits, like a sleepwalker on his way through the night, overtook them and left them behind.

At half past five, an alarm clock rang in the neighbouring compartment. The journalist woke with a start and had his wife give him a tablet to calm him down. The surgeon disappeared between the compartments to smoke, and the women with the friendship bracelets returned from the train toilet in tight-fitting clothes, surrounded by a scent cloud of toothpaste and deodorant, so they could enjoy the space and stretch out one last time, staring out in silence at the factory sites they were passing through. Shortly after six, they crossed the Rhine. Bunches of locks of different sizes and types hung on the railings of the railway bridge, and the journalist said something about the German sense for romantic gestures, at which the women with the friendship bracelets shot caustic looks at one another.

The sun cast a cold morning light on the square in front of Cologne railway station. In the long shadow of the cathedral, the boy shared the first joint of his life with the surgeon. The connecting train to Brussels departed from platform three and smelt of upholstery cleaning agents and fresh coffee; the boy felt pleasantly tired at last. He rested his head on the green-and-white crane and had already fallen asleep as the train pulled out. He passed Aachen station and the border posts in Liège-Guillemins without being checked again and only woke up when the train slid into Bruxelles-Midi in complete silence.

Standing under the great dome of the station, he leant his head back to follow the acrobatic arc of a pigeon through the clean Belgian air of the station, until he became dizzy. He just managed to catch the express train to Marseilles-Saint-Charles, the doors gave the signal and silently closed behind his backpack. Almost all the seats in the open compartment were occupied. Nobody was talking. Newspapers rustled, buttons clicked, a hint of music from the headphones of a little dark-skinned man in a pinstripe suit who held his Walkman like a raw egg in his muscular hands. The boy removed his backpack awkwardly and set it down, sinking into a purple-cushioned window seat, marked first class, though he didn't notice that at first.

There is not much more to report about this first long journey. The boy spoke to no one and no one spoke to the boy. It was the middle of the day and everyone was preoccupied with themselves. Only the man in the pinstripe suit sitting diagonally across from him, a professional boxer in the flyweight category from Marseilles, every so often fell to gazing at the white laces in his combat boots, the close-cropped hair, the broad shoulders under his bomber jacket, the weird backpack with the crane emblem in the luggage rack. Something about this boy looked anything but Nazi, but the boxer couldn't put his finger on it. Arsehole or not, he wondered, *salaud ou quoi*, sink or swim with someone . . . like him?

The boy registered none of this. He had rested his forehead against the window. No one approached him about his second-class ticket. He saw the planes taking off over Paris Charles de Gaulle, lifting into the air and disappearing into the August sky; he saw the *bon voyage* drawn in great sweeping letters in the dust on the glazed outer wall of the station at Marne-la-Vallée–Chessy; he saw the midday heat over the greenhouses beyond Lyon, the rows of trees behind the noise barrier along the Autoroute du Sud which flashed up from time to time next to the tracks like the thought of the complete impossibility of turning round now; he saw the poplars that gradually turned into cypresses, cypresses and broom, on the hills of the Massif Central that became drier the further he went. Nothing here looked like the Europe he knew, and yet he was in the middle of it all, as though in the silent eye of a hurricane. Onwards he went, crossing the country southwards. He left behind the barren plateaus of the Cévennes, the grey villages of basalt and glass and the heavy motionless thunderclouds of this late-summer day, beneath which the train shot along, white and silver, until the villages could only be seen as a haze on the horizon; he detached his head from the window, surprised by the bright green of the pine trees, and also by the growing form of the Montagne Sainte-Victoire, the stone of which supposedly had a different hue every day and which was clearly visible from his new place of residence. And then he was there.

He got up, buckled his East Elbe District Transport Company backpack onto his back and stepped out into the corridor where a Black man in a pinstripe suit glared at him sharply. The boy averted his gaze and let him go ahead, because avoiding trouble was another skill he had perfected years ago. His combat boots were part of this strategy, but in a way that he himself hardly understood. Clumsily but silently he made his way through the large open compartment to the train door.

These were the last few metres during which the boy felt completely himself. That didn't occur to him particularly at the time. But by the time he had left the platform, he was just another exhausted passenger arriving. Later he would be a *salaud de Nazi*. The stubborn boy with the inadequate vocabulary, the East German colossus in combat boots, Germanic child-giant, a case, a traumatized hobgoblin and other things besides. For his parents, he would simply be *our successful son travelling abroad*.

‡

When is she coming? I ask.

She's coming tomorrow, says Maman.

Maman stirs the spoon in her coffee. It is black and stinks. Maman has small eyes. Maman always drinks coffee when she has small eyes. Coffee makes you happy, she says. But not right now. She tucks a blonde strand of hair behind her ear. Her hair hangs lifeless from her head.

How many more hours? I ask.

Go back to sleep, says Maman.

Her little eyes are a bit swollen. Coffee makes you beautiful, she says. Maman would love to be beautiful for Papa. But she is not.

Papa still sometimes says: But you're beautiful to me.

Then Maman always says: Not beautiful enough, it seems. She doesn't say it now, because Papa isn't there. The voices are just in my head.

Go back to sleep, Maman says in real life.

Yes, I say. But how many hours?

2

So, there he is standing in front of a coin-operated telephone in the railway station of a southern French town close to Marseilles, and his school French still does not extend beyond *The Little Prince*. That's why he doesn't immediately understand what Madame says on the phone: Oh, I see? That's a surprise! Monsieur had searched the entire station and had just come back home. They hadn't been aware that—*mais bon*, he hears Madame say at the other end, accompanied by a harrumph that is difficult to interpret. Monsieur would pick him up in half an hour.

He replaces the handset, pockets the coins and looks round. The big wide world looks remarkably like a small-town station. A rather unspectacular small-town station. Flower shop, newspaper kiosk, ticket counter, public toilet. Out through the automatic glass doors, he steps into the open air. Tufts of cloud hang on invisible cords above the yellow station facade, and above them a pristine sky stretches away. Plane trees line the streets below. Parked cars, a moped honking, a lady in a sand-coloured blazer crossing the street. The boy does not put the backpack down and remains directly under the red-and-white illuminated sign for SNCF. The glass door behind him opens and closes, he is standing in the way and hears a remark from behind him he does not understand, but he does not move from the spot. What on earth is he thinking? He is thinking of the high cornfields behind the new build of his childhood. What is corn in French anyway? When he closes his eyes, he hears the blood roaring in his ears, as if he were standing on the Elbe Bridge, at rush hour, in the middle of his homeland, which he doesn't care about, but which is still his reference point for everything.

Thirty-five minutes later, Monsieur parks in the station fore-court, gets out with the engine still running and opens the boot. The boy has now come up with a few words: *enchanté*. I hope I haven't made you to any—all jumbled up. He has never seen a Lexus LS up close and has certainly never sat in one. This one shimmers dark green and a touch too clean, which is also the only thing it has in common with the other vehicles, sounding their horns in a restrained way on the roundabout in front of the station forecourt. Monsieur doesn't seem to be listening at all, and on the way home speaks with gentle determination, without even pausing for breath. Occasionally he points at a building or a fountain. The boy tries to keep his eyes open and nods occasionally. His employer's hands are neat and delicate; they remind him of the surgeon's hands on the night train to Cologne. He wears a signet ring on his right ring finger. He holds the steering wheel with the fingertips of his left hand, as if he were steering for fun.

Although he barely looks, the boy will later remember every detail of this trip to the house. The unnaturally blue sky behind the tinted windshield, the equally unnatural-looking cypresses to the right and left of the expressway, cyclists with helmets, he has never seen cyclists with helmets, at least . . . maybe on television on the Tour de France, the French signs, the abrupt descent, the steep road down into the village. And because Monsieur has the windows down, he will also remember the sound of the engine as it moves through the empty little streets and over speed bumps, he has never seen speed bumps. He will also remember the limestone walls in front of the different plots of land, the pine trees in the front gardens, the hedges and walls in front of them. The names of the villas are written on the front gates: Maison de l'Ecureuille, Maison du Renard, Maison Jules. A single gate is open. Through it he sees a neglected garden, a large magpie, sitting motionless on the edge of a bird bath and looking directly into his eyes. Next to the bird is a man standing equally motionless in the tall grass: with white hair and a cigarillo in the corner of his mouth. They carry on uphill.

The plots are getting bigger, the walls are imperceptibly higher. Lawn sprinklers. No dogs barking, no kids screaming, no music. At the end of this street, the Lexus moves down a gear and turns into a residential area of large, newly renovated villas. Except for them, no one is out on the street. He sees flat shingle roofs of the kind you see in an advert for Provence and shutters, many of them closed—the boy also remembers that. The automatic engine switches down again, Monsieur looks at him sideways and brakes in front of a closed steel gate. A keypad has been inserted into the pink lime-washed wall beside it.

‡

It's today. She arrives today. She's almost here. She will take everything away. She will take away Maman's little eyes. Not her eyes. Only that they are so small and swollen. She will take away the bruises too. I won't say who here has bruises. I won't even say it to myself.

She will have long hair. And big, steel-blue eyes. Steel is not blue. But steel is the toughest metal in the world, Lionel says. Lionel is my brother. He is already ten and knows about these things. Lionel was there when Papa and Maman met. Papa loves Lionel. I think he finds him more beautiful than Maman.

Steel-blue, yes. Her steel-blue gaze turns everything into ice. That's how I picture it. Maybe our au pair will be called Gerda. Like in Maïes's book about the Snow Queen. I want to be down in the courtyard when she arrives. But Lionel is holding on to my arm.

Now they're coming off the highway, he says. His fingers on my arm are white from holding so tight. Now they are in the village, says Lionel.

You're so stupid, I say.

Now they're coming up the mountain, says Lionel.

You're such a worm, I say.

Now they are . . .

I don't listen any more. I listen to hear what is going on outside. Another ten minutes, says Lionel.

My arm has fallen asleep.

Now they're stopping at the gate, says Lionel.

A car is really stopping in front of the house.

Now Papa is typing the code into the key . . .

The courtyard gate opens. Lionel lets me go. I yelp.

We jump off the bed. We rush outside.

The car door is open. Where is the au pair, where is she? A man is standing by the boot, he reaches in and lifts out a battered backpack. He doesn't look like Gerda. Not even like Kai. His shaved head reflects the sun.

There must be a mistake, Maman mutters behind us. They have sent us the wrong one.

3

Monsieur hops lightly out of the car, leans against the wall with one hand, taps a code in with the other, and when he sits back in the car and the two halves of the gate slowly part, he looks over at him again. But now the boy is too tired to talk in French about how impressive he finds the thing with the entrance gate. Monsieur looks away, revs one last time and rolls into the large, freshly raked yard.

He will remember everything, every detail of their first trip to the house. Just not arriving. Later, he will scour his memory for details without finding much. Was Madame standing in the yard when he got out of the car? What had they said to each other and what had they understood? Had they shaken hands, kissed each other on the cheek? Were Maud and Lionel there? And if so, how had they reacted? He will not recall. Even the faces of Monsieur and Madame will be two blurred shapes in his memory, with sentences hurtling out at high speed, to which he nods and declares himself *d'accord*. It is as if in that first half hour he had agreed to all kinds of arrangements that he never would have signed up to, had they been said in his mother tongue.

His employers, on the other hand, would later tell the agency on the phone that it had all been quite a surprise. But they had given the, well, the young man a warm welcome and shown him the house. That was all they could do, after all, wasn't it? It had all gone almost as they had imagined, almost as desired, you might say. Almost. Except for the boy himself, whose appearance had made such an impression that they could hardly imagine having him here for more than a week, let alone entrusting the children to him for a single day. What sort of impression? The agency would be happy to send out a colleague to ascertain with their own eyes that this young man looks like . . . like a Nazi. *Un vrai salaud de Nazi*, one might say. But they would cope with someone like him. Oh yes. That they would. Goodbye.

His memories set in again with the moment he closes the door of the attic behind him. Inside there is an empty, dark cupboard, the door creaks when opened. Next a wooden box, the lid of which he carefully lifts: it is also empty. A small desk with an oblique writing surface, which he also opens, but there are no letters from former au pairs in it, and that somehow makes him feel better. He already knows that he will not sit at this desk, his thighs hardly fit underneath. On the window side of the room, he cannot stand upright without hitting his head against the gables. As everywhere, he feels out of place here too, but it does not matter. Finally, a bed of heavy, almost black wood. He stretches out, taking care not to crumple the bedspread. How many au pairs have been here before him? This is his last thought before he falls, still fully dressed, into a deep and dreamless sleep until the next morning. He does not even notice Maud and Lionel, who quietly turn the door handle before going to bed, stand at the edge of his bed and examine his pale face for a long time.

What's going on now? asked Matusja. She was standing by his bed, bewildered once again as to what was wrong with him. The footsteps of Viktor's sister and her husband were still echoing through the quiet of the night-time hallway. Lately, the two of them always rushed to get out of the apartment as soon as Viktor's parents were back. As if they did not want to hang around. What was wrong with wanting to have the occasional toast with her step-daughter and her charming husband? She was not a *machekha*, not an evil stepmother. Then they would have more life in the house, more family, if only on the German side. But why shouldn't young people get on with enjoying their lives? Matusja understood her own son even less. What was wrong with him? What was going on with their Viktor, who, every time they had been out, would sit for days in front of the living room wall unit, as if he wanted to crawl inside it, simply watching TV. He stared palely at the screen and watched the endless parade for the fortieth anniversary of the GDR, as if it were a funeral procession. It was not as if they left the boy home alone, his sister and her husband were always there to look after him. And should an eleven-year-old, look so, so . . . old? Even when he was asleep, with the moon globe switched on and tucked under his pale arm like a doll?

From the hallway, Matusja heard her husband turn the key to the apartment door. What is it now, he asked, lumbering towards the children's room, still in his good shoes. She quickly pulled the blanket over Viktor. Oh, she muttered, carefully lifting the globe out of Viktor's limp arms, look at him.

That boy of ours is moon-mad! His father laughed softly and drew Matusja close. One day he will be a strapping cosmonaut!

But the mood did not seem to lift, so they stood by the bed next to their stubborn little son for a while longer examining his sleeping face. Goodness knows what he would get up to if they did not have his sister and her nice husband, Matusja told herself.

Setting the lunar globe neatly back on the bedside table and switching it off, they crept out of his room. Viktor rubbed his eyes and turned over to stare out into the darkness of space behind the window. How many children before him had been fucked by their own sister's husband?

4

The sixth, says Madame. You are the sixth au pair to be with our family. The children are quite used to it, Maud doesn't know it any other way.

It is quiet in the house. Maud and Lionel are at school, Monsieur in his office in Marseilles. Madame is sitting stiffly at the dining room table, and is, given the circumstances, remarkably reticent, but what is there to say since this strange boy with his lack of vocabulary doesn't understand a word anyway? He is looking at the white moons under her short, well-groomed fingernails. But you're not . . . she adds, as if she has only now noticed, and slides her hands from the table. He nods and heaps two spoonfuls of sugar into his coffee. The cup is too small for his hand. He tries not to rattle the spoon as he stirs and feels Madame's little dark-grey eyes boring through him. What do you have to say about this?

But what is there to say? At the interview the person in charge of the applications in Dresden, a big, busty deaconess with the thickest varifocals in the world, had pointed out to him gently that girls would have a better chance of getting a job as an au pair. So, he had written the name Viktoria on the application form. It differed from his own name only by two letters, so was a trifle compared to the other lies on his slate. It was also the name of Ruth's mother. An auspicious adjustment to the facts, that the deaconess had either not noticed or had kindly let pass. But, of course, he can't say that.

Or had the whole thing been a madness? He feels too clumsy for the espresso cup, the spoon, the creaking wooden chair underneath him. But surely this is better than cruising through the villages in Marcel's car, bellowing *Berlin! Berlin! We're going to Berlin!* without ever even getting to the outer edge of the S-Bahn? Berlin is no longer my capital city, his father had muttered, reaching across the dinner table into the wall unit and switching off the daily news. And the glory days long gone, Matusja had sighed, sweeping away his hand to look for a channel that would be showing the landing of the Russian cosmonauts Zibliev and Lasutkin after their disappointing series of breakdowns in the Mir space station. In his mind, Viktor sees his parents standing in front of the wall unit, shaking their ageing heads over a present that, in their eyes, consists only of failure. But is this not better than coming home every day to find all the rejection letters that Matusja has neatly stacked on his old childhood desk—Dear Mr So-and-so, due to your miserable Abitur grade, you can, unfortunately, not train as a cook in our hotel chain, we wish you a nice life—? Viktor thinks of his half-sister, who will soon be having a baby and is now always there, sitting on the couch at home, with the insolent grin of children from broken homes, who are always the ones to get their arses spoiled rotten. Who gets their arse spoiled rotten is my business, his shit-for-brains brother-in-law had once said in front of the assembled family, and his half-sister had laughed tightly and changed the subject. Anything is better than that, Viktor thinks, without having words for it. Father's look behind the rimless lenses of his reading glasses as he placed the results of the army aptitude test on the dinner plate. Psychologically unstable.

Nonsense, his father had muttered. Complete nonsense, all this so as not to have to serve our country, not even community service.

What do you care, I thought it wasn't your country any longer! Viktor had roared and slammed the front door behind him. Unstable. Had he trained at the gymnastics club for years, only to be classed as unstable now? Had he cleaned up this low-life club with Marcel and the others for nothing, only to be considered unstable now? Germany! he had growled at the empty house fronts along his street. But Germany was like the dear Lord in Ruth's family, who always knew everything but never answered.

That night Viktor had hung about in front of her house for a while. Did her mother still wear the salt-dough cross? Light fell from the windows onto the empty street underneath a summer night sky crisscrossed by the Perseids, Mare Serenitatis and Mare Imbrium lending a crushed face to the moon. Ruth didn't seem to hear any of the pebbles he threw up against the window. If anyone was mentally unstable here, it was her! What with all the vampire films and the music, these beautiful, emotionally cold attic serenades. After his fifth beer Viktor tried again with bigger stones. When the pane cracked, he turned around and wandered slowly, far too slowly, down the road towards the football field.

Anything is better than that, he thinks now. Cooking, how about that? Like his Matusja, preferably twice a day. Quails and quiche and all sorts of things he can't even pronounce yet. And yes, he would shake out the beds. He would even remember how to pronounce the names of the children. And everything else too.

Sche veux, he tries and looks down at his ripped biceps. He feels like a yeti in a human igloo. I want, he thinks, everything. Anything but back. He lifts his shaved head and responds to Madame's wobbly smile with a wrinkled grin. Then he raises the index and middle finger of his right hand to make the peace sign and says something he thinks is the right answer to Madame's question: *Sche veux garder vos enfants très bon.*

5

So, what happens now? says Madame. This question is not directed at Viktor, but at the head of the au pair agency in Marseilles, a woman with pleasant curly hair and a firm handshake, who is sitting at an overloaded desk working on her tax return and has quite different concerns than the gender and brand of shoe of one of her charges. Well, he is not unfriendly, exactly, says Madame, he is certainly making an effort. But, of course, it's just not possible. They had been expecting a young girl, *une jeune fille*, and now there was this East German giant in combat boots hanging about the house. He simply couldn't stay on, could he? The children would be frightened. No, they hadn't said that explicitly. But they were pale and quiet, especially the boy, and it wasn't anything to do with her! I can assure you, says Madame into the rustle of paper on the other end of the line, the stubborn boy with the lack of vocabulary can spend a week here, but she and her husband will never, ever, allow him to supervise the children alone! Goodbye.

Nothing lasts as long as temporary arrangements. The East German giant is here, after all, and the children have to go to school. Viktor, who barely gives his arrival just two days ago a second thought jumps out of bed. The last traces of the joint from Cologne railway station have disappeared. When he comes downstairs, Monsieur is just driving off on his Italian MV Agusta with its tubular frame, the courtyard gravel spurting up against the red bodywork. Madame is jammed in the door with the phone squashed between shoulder and ear, soothing her first patient, who is already waiting in front of the practice, while she buttons up the little one's cardigan. Madame's 'psycho-studio', as Monsieur calls it, is located on the ground floor, but has a separate entrance with a bell all too audible from upstairs, which has just started ringing again. Victoire, calls Madame emphasising the last syllable. Victoire, *on a besoin de toi*! Someone has to go with the children. They have to go through this piece of forest, and there is sometimes someone hanging about there, whom she doesn't trust an inch—if he gets her drift. Lionel knows the way. Surely he will manage that, what does he reckon, Victoire?

Viktor shakes the limp hands of Maud and Lionel, who seem to find this hilarious; turns a deaf ear to the highspeed barrage of chirruped comments, which he does not understand in any case; and, because he can't think of anything better, introduces himself to them again in all formality. *Salut, ça va? Je m'appelle Viktor.* Why on earth this should prompt the next salvo of laugher, he has no idea. The three of them ignore Madame's nervous blinking and set off.

Did everything go well? she asks later. His broad shoulders almost fill the frame of the kitchen door. How unnatural, she finds herself thinking, disconcerted, and squints past Viktor into the kitchen. The ceramic hob and work surfaces are completely crumb-free in a way they have not been for months. She tries not to think of the butler of the Addams Family, what was his name again—*you rang*? And you had a nice chat on the way too? Viktor's face creases into a baffled smile. Not exactly confidence-inspiring.

Today it has rung a lot, he replies, as if he had read her thoughts. *Eh ben, oui*, she says, and cannot help herself; she bursts out laughing. The laughter swells in small, flat bubbles from her mouth, oh, hehehe, and moves towards Viktor, as if of its own volition *oh, excuse moi ha-haha*! In other words, Madame laughs away all her fear of this Teutonic child-giant. This is not something that will be repeated often, but she cannot take it back. And by the time she has finally shown Viktor the whole house and explained all his tasks, morning, noon and the early afternoon have passed, and Madame thaws and becomes talkative . . .

Monday ironing. The underwear, as well, please Victoire, then it can be folded. Anything that is not for ironing, please fold as well. We have a special technique for socks and underwear, if you would please use it too, Victoire. I'll demonstrate it for you: first so, so and then so, do you see? On Tuesdays, the two bathrooms and the lavatories need to be cleaned. And at the end you polish the tiles with this little cloth, so they sparkle. Cooking on Wednesdays. Maud and Lionel stay at home that day, so you spend the day with them. Thursdays all three floors need hoovering. My husband has had this special suction system installed in the walls, you plug this hose end into the connection here on the wall, turn on this switch next to it, and all the dust is sucked down by a pipe system between the walls into a tank in the basement, you didn't know that such a thing existed, right, Victoire? On Fridays you drive to the city and get fresh ravioli at the Italian shop. The first time you can go with the *femme de ménage* so you know the way. Then ironing again and folding. Always make the children's beds in the morning, please. You don't have bedspreads like this in East Germany, do you? You must tuck them in at the foot of the bed frames and then pull them *très*, *très* smooth and flat. I think the standard of a good hotel should be maintained in the home too. In the morning you should always cook ready for the evening. The *femme de ménage* will help you for the first month, Victoire, but after that you will manage our recipes on your own. Oh, ha ha, someone is very happy, who would have thought it. Oh yes, and take care of the children every afternoon. This is of course your real job with us, Victoire. Not the cooking! Do you actually understand anything I'm saying? Victoire?

6

As the steel gate closes silently behind him that afternoon, his head is whirling with the words he has just heard: *emmener*, or was it *amener, plier le linge, couvre-lit, femme de ménage*, cleaning lady, maybe, or housekeeper, probably doesn't matter. Viktor walks up the street between the villas. The pavement slabs are smooth and hot, there is already a smell of summer and salt from the pools behind the houses. The high walls cast cool shadows on the pavement. Behind the last house, the road turns and passes through a piece of woodland that Madame said he had to cross, just follow his nose, she said, and he would soon see the primary school, or did she mean something else? Cool forest air hangs between the trees like freshly laundered washing, the tarmac road is dark and warm, from time to time cars go past with a subdued purr, the children on the back seat turn to look at him for some inexplicable reason. Then he is alone again. Halfway through, he overtakes an elderly gentleman, who immediately snaps to attention and raises a hand to his wispy grey hair as if in a military salute. *Vos chaussures*, General, Sir! he calls out, or has Viktor misunderstood? When he finally comes out in a car park, he turns round again. The man is still standing between the pine trees looking back at him, his crooked palms pressed to his trouser seams.

With the deliberate casualness of the newcomer, he crosses the car park passing between convertibles and coupés; a Facel Vega is parked at the very edge, just like that, and there are occasional squeaky-clean Mini Coopers. The entrance gate of the École du Forêt is open. Slim mothers in roll-neck sweaters stand huddled in little groups laughing, school bags hanging on their wrists in tasteful colours; between them, girls with long ponytails and boys in short-sleeved shirts. There is the occasional father too, badminton bags hung over one shoulder while they lift up their children like light, empty vessels on the other shoulder, and stroll across the car park, bouncing along the forest path in their trainers. At last Viktor looks down at himself. His feet are dark grey with summer dust, on the right instep an encrusted spot of some indefinable colour, his soles spotted black with tar. His combat boots were too hot for him in the summer heat, he left them in the house. Man, he thinks. This is where you work.

When he raises his head again, he is greeted with a round face laughing into his. A shock of tousled black hair, a red mouth and between the incisors a small gap of the kind that makes it impossible for you to look elsewhere. This tooth-gap belongs to Julija. And although she has not yet revealed her name, in less than a minute it will seem to him that he has always known it.

She: You're barefoot.

He: (nods)

She: Did you know you don't seem to have any shoes on?

He: (nods)

She: Are you picking up Lionel and Maud?

He: (nods)

She: Look, here they come. I am the au pair from next door.

He: (nods)

She: Your French isn't very good, is it?

He: (nods)

She: Don't worry, it'll come. I am . . .

Julija. Viktor has never heard this name, but he has not grown up in Ukraine, where millions of girls are called that. But he recognizes her accent. Her *r* rolled with the tip of her tongue on her palate, the soft singing of her questions, the casual smattering of sounds tumbling from her red mouth that make the world shrink before him and sound familiar and strange at the same time. As if he had already known Julija when he was still chasing through the cornfield behind his new-build block. Julija, then. Although he is the only one far and wide not wearing plimsolls, and worse, not wearing any shoes at all, and although two children are approaching, by whom he must at all costs be accepted in order for him to be able to do his job, and although, what is more, he is not sure whether the girl with the melodious name is laughing at him, he suddenly feels better.

A little awkwardly, he pats Maud and Lionel on the shoulders. All of them set off, past badminton bags and

Chevrolets, past the old man at the edge of the car park, whom the children happily greet, because it is Jim who has been absent for a whole summer as he has been fighting in goodness knows what battle.

Maud and Lionel go ahead, closely followed by a six-year-old with tight curls who desperately wants to know why they are in such a hurry until Julija stuffs a wholegrain biscuit into his mouth. Her short hair sways as she bounces along and the gap in her teeth becomes visible, when Viktor finally manages to open his mouth and says in Ukrainian: Oh my God, it's crazy that you and I are here together . . . The familiar words of his mother tongue tumble from his mouth, as if he were still the little boy with a wrinkled smile and a moon globe at home, he has so far only spoken Ukrainian with his Matusja, and once a year with the family in Ternopil. But it does not matter.

He is in the middle of a new phase of his story, and that is a good thing. Slowly, Julija and Viktor follow their employers' children across the cool, needle-strewn forest floor towards their houses.

This peaceful state of affairs does not last long. It ends right in front of the steel gate that leads to the courtyard. The second Julija has disappeared behind the wall to the next property with the curly-headed child in tow, Lionel and Maud turn to him. Maud puts her head on one side and examines him. Lionel shoves his hands in his trouser pockets and looks just past Viktor. You want to know something? he says. You have exactly two weeks.

Two weeks? Viktor is still smiling.

By then, you'll be gone. I don't need anyone to look after me. Lionel turns away and taps a code into the keypad on the wall. Facing the closed steel gate, he adds: I'm not afraid. Without looking back the boy disappears through the widening gap between the steel gates and into the courtyard.

Why afraid, thinks Viktor and looks down at his body. Afraid of me? His big hands hang limply by his sides. Under his toenails he can see dust from the forest. Let them be afraid of him at home. Anyone who wants to look into his heart, including Ruth, should be afraid. If you're afraid of someone, you can't fuck them. But here? Maud has stopped next to Viktor. She scratches her nose. Her hand is covered with felt-tip pen ink. She looks up at him and screws her eyes. You're not a girl at all, she says. He shakes his head, still smiling, but it feels kind of stiff. Maud puts her hands on her hips. And you snore. Then she turns around and stomps across the yard into the house.

Viktor stays where he is for a while until he also goes through the steel gate which is now wide open. Under his bare feet he feels the sharp edges of the snow-white gravel, which has stayed cool despite the sun.

Maman and I are lying in my bed. We have pulled the blanket over our heads. It is stuffy underneath. But everything else is outside, and that's what it's all about. Okay, almost everything. Maman believes I can't fall asleep without her. Really, it's the other way around.

What are we going to do about him? I ask.

Nothing, she says. He can stay. Since he is already here anyway.

Maman is not a fighter, that much is clear.

What does au pair mean? I want to know.

Maman buries her face in my hair.

That means he's here to take care of you, she says. That's why he's learning our language.

So, our au pair girl is a boy. I just say au pair. With the emphasis on the second syllable, like au secours. It's a pity Jim isn't our au pair. He would help, he would fight.

And the au pair? His hair is shaved so short that you can see right into his ears. He looks like the opposite of Gerda. When he laughs his face is all creased. Like the bedcover over us.

I don't think he gets what is going on here. I tested it out. Lionel's bed is right next to mine. All that separates our two rooms is the wall between them. Maman lies in my bed. Papa lies in Lionel's.

I put music on in Lionel's room. Then close the door and go up to the au pair's room. Door open, in, door closed. Window open: legs dangling out over the roof tiles. The way he always does it when he thinks we're all in our rooms. You can't hear anything from the window. Nothing at all.

Now Maman and I lie under the blanket whispering.

What are they doing?

They're doing sums.

Why aren't they talking?

Because they're doing sums.

But why is Lionel crying?

No answer. Maman breathes deeply and evenly into my hair. I can't breathe. In the next room Lionel in crying. Whenever we need someone to fight, Maman falls asleep.

And Jim? Jim lives in the house next door, so far away. Maybe he doesn't need us though.

In the next room, Lionel is crying. I can't breathe.

You don't know the shoe-fac? Marcel asked. The butterfly knife swirling in front of him in the smoky air and cutting it into shreds.

Viktor and the others were standing at the bus stop by the football pitch sharing a packet of Lucky Strike. The lawn in front of them was surrounded by red metal pipes, where the wind made strange whistling sounds, like the boat masts of an abandoned harbour. The windows of the sports club were dark; today's game had been cancelled. Not on the ninth of November, the coach had said, and now some of them were standing at the bus stop, where Marcel and his gang normally stood and cheered.

Man, the shoe factory, said Marcel and flicked his glowing stub across the goal. My old man used to work there. Lighters clicked, murmuring, a girl with a shaved neck and plucked eyebrows laughed at something. Proper German workmanship, Marcel said undeterred, not the Vietnamese-made crap you get today. Bored, the girl turned to Marcel. But now there's a club for lefty scum in there, he said. The Kirchendiebe and other indie low-lives play there—that punk band, the

Beatsteaks, were there once and other sorts of degenerate music. Murmurs of agreement. People who snort coke and everything. Someone whistled through their fingers. Someone else laughed and placed a small light-blue pill on his tongue. Crack, Marcel blurted. All that corrosive poison from Poland, set to ruin our country, is stashed there.

Hey, be quiet, called the girl, Marcel wants to tell you something.

There's a party there tonight, said Marcel and stretched out his arms. Everyone's going. All the scum, the punks, the dopeheads, the high-school students. He put his arm round Viktor, who had towered over him for a long time now. Of course, not the decent high-school students like our good Ukrainian here, Marcel said and laughed. He was the only one who was not completely wrong about Viktor's lineage. Meanwhile the girl with the plucked eyebrows moved round and stood in front of them. She drew on her cigarette and blew the smoke into Marcel and Viktor's faces. Her feathered hair almost covered her darkly made-up eyes. And? she asked.

Marcel lifted his arms. His watch shimmered in the dim light of the overcast afternoon. Well, we're going too, he shouted at the group. We're going to have a bit of fun.

It was almost one o'clock in the morning as the cars pulled up in front of the iron gate that led down to the factory hall on the industrial tracks. *It's time to act, time to act*, growled a Stuka song from the loudspeakers of the Golf, where Viktor sat in the back seat, sandwiched between two mates of similar stature. *Germany must change. Germany will change*! In the boot, the petrol bombs clattered in the beer crates: hours had been spent on handicrafts. Time to give 'em hell, Marcel had said at some point and handed out the baseball bats from his private store. Viktor had weighed his in his hand, impressed by the heft and the grain—like on an old musical instrument. The girl with the shaved neck was at the wheel. Let's party, she had said as Viktor got out of the car with the others, but don't hang about. When the cops come, us up here will be off!

Viktor felt the exhaust fumes from the running engines warm on the back of his neck as he went down the narrow staircase behind the gate into the club grounds, following Marcel and the others. Downstairs it looked a mess. Fairy lights were strung through the trees and scrubby bushes; there was scum everywhere perching on the crumbling walls and old beams with their tangled hairstyles, dense smoke rising from their open mouths. In the corner was a large bonfire, where they crowded round laughing and shoving who knows what down their throats, as Viktor saw in the dim light. Not far away two girls with long hair stood in the bushes snogging. They kept their eyes closed as Viktor and the others pushed past them to the entrance. That's when the baseball bats came out of the jackets. The doorman, an old acquaintance of Marcel's, just had time to shout *fucking Nazis* before blood spurted from his face. As he lay on his side, cowering under Marcel's attack, Viktor clambered over him. Inside, the ceiling was hung with military netting containing countless shoes. They reminded him of a school visit to Buchenwald, where he had used his ability developed years earlier to flip an inner switch and feel nothing at all. Viktor had already flipped this useful switch in the girl's car, so that he could now shout with glee: It looks like a concentration camp in here.

They smashed up the club. They swept the bottles from the bar, sending splinters of glass flying into the air. They jumped over the bar and trampled the decadent cocktail mixers, crushed the test tubes for the Bloody Marys and poured the contents of the cash register into the outdoor toilet at the back exit. It wasn't about the money. It wasn't about the principle either. But in the backs curled before him, the arms raised in defence and the centrifugal power of the baseball bat in Viktor's hand lay something that came pretty close to his idea of joy.

Until he saw the dance floor. Despite the almost complete darkness, he recognized Ruth immediately. She stood on the edge swaying slightly, lost in the rhythmic beat that still emanated from the loudspeakers, even though the DJ had long since scarpered. It was some kind of cover version of this old Malaria! song, *cold clear water*, coming towards him from the speakers, while Ruth's slender figure leant forward and moved slightly to the monotonous beat, as if nothing else in the world existed. She had shorter hair now that fell to one side as she danced, revealing her eyes. Viktor paused and walked closer. Strobe lights lit up the dance floor in jerky flashes, so that Ruth looked different with each beat, a flip book with pages missing. *Over my hands*, a woman's voice sang, Ruth's fingernails still looked just as bitten as they had been when they used to bake salt dough together in a previous life, *over my arms, over my shoulders*, her ears are fine and yet she doesn't even get that the rooms in front are being taken apart? *Over my legs, over my thighs*, he looked at Ruth like he had never looked at her before, not during their rare meetings in the school playground and not years before, when he didn't have a friend like Marcel and she had the most beautiful mother in the world. For the first time, he looked at her like a stranger looking at a stranger. As if each of her movements were directed towards him. Beneath her plaid shirt were amazing breasts that swayed softly to the beat, *over my breast, I close my eyes*! When he finally stood behind the abandoned DJ's booth and ripped the plug out, Ruth stopped abruptly and looked around. Except for them, there was no one left in the room. With the speakers silent, the crashing and groaning from the other rooms was suddenly deafening. In the chill-out zone there was a noise like New Year's Eve fireworks; from the VIP room came bright ceiling light and curses, because Marcel was in there, slitting open the mattresses, in search of the good stuff; from somewhere came the sound of glass shattering. Arms hanging by her sides, Ruth stood on the edge of the empty dance floor and stared at Viktor in surprise. What he wanted to do was hide her in his bomber jacket. Piss off, man, make yourself scarce, he shouted at her. But she didn't piss off.

Slowly she crossed the dance floor. The strobe light was still on. Jerkily she went up behind the DJ's desk and stood in front of Viktor. She reached up to his shoulder. Her breasts were only a hair's breadth away from him. So now, she said calmly, you are one of them too.

Then she turned on her heel and calmly left the club, walked across the chillout zone with mosquito netting hanging down from the ceiling, past a burning Molotov cocktail. Viktor's joy was gone. Ruth! Wait! By the time he came round and stumbled after her, Ruth was gone.

Viktor stepped outside. The night had become colder. A piece of moon hung half torn-down from the sky. The yard was swept clean, snogging couples and scum—you couldn't see them for dust. Not much time seemed to have passed, as the cars were still standing at the top of the road with their engines running, the campfire was burning. In the glow of the flames, Viktor caught sight of a movement. There was a guy lying in a pool of his own vomit. Had probably had too much even before they'd gone in. Viktor became conscious of the hard, warm wood of the baseball bat in his hand. The guy's black-dyed mohawk lay spread out on the wooden bench, where he lay sleeping like a baby. He was older, Viktor reckoned him to be twenty-five, the same age as his bastard of a brother-in-law.

Viktor lifted a boot and nailed the fan of hair to the bench with his heel. When his first blow landed in the man's belly, the punk opened his eyes and moaned. With the monotonous regularity of a machine, Viktor swung the baseball bat down on the cowering shape before him, his arms still crossed over his head, howling and spitting, but Viktor kept on mechanically thudding into his stomach, knee and chest until the guy just whimpered and then was so still that he could clearly hear the quiet click of the switch inside him, which turned back and then it was nice and quiet inside as well.

Are you off your head? Marcel screamed behind him and grabbed him by the collar to pull him off the slumped shape. You'll fucking kill him! He grabbed Viktor by the neck and shoved him up the stairs, where the others were waiting in the cars. They put their foot down to accelerate away and were already fishing the first beer bottles out of the boot, in celebration of this successful clean-up operation, as the girl with the plucked brows called it. But they could not get the good mood back. And while Marcel stared straight ahead and wiped his big hand across his face, and the silence in Viktor's head passed imperceptibly into a low rumble and Marcel said: Shit, you always go too far, which Viktor didn't quite catch because of the noise, the damp night air came in through the open car window and stroked their sweaty faces, or were they tears, but that couldn't be. They were about to cross the Elbe Bridge when they heard the sirens. Well, about time, Marcel muttered, they're going to take care of it. Viktor wound the window up again, the other girl pressed Play. *It's time to act, time to act,* came the whine from the speakers in the boot behind them, *Germany must change, Germany will change.* But it sounded very different from the way it had on the way there.

8

From the closed door of Lionel's room comes the thud of French hip-hop. Maud's door is open, she is not visible herself, but behind the kitchen, just by the pool, there are small footprints drying in the July sun. Viktor wanders around the kitchen flicking through his travel dictionary to translate the recipes Madame has left on the counter for him. At almost half past five he hears quick steps in the living room, in the stairwell, right behind his back in the kitchen, but whenever he turns round, Maud is already gone. Just before six, as he starts washing the salad for dinner, he catches sight of her out of the corner of his eye: she is standing barefoot in a bathing suit in the open patio door, watching him.

Time passes in this way. The summer holidays are in full swing, but the children have been signed up for endless summer courses. Swimming and drama for Maud, computer and graffiti for Lionel (education is important, Victoire). In the mornings Viktor sits on his bed fully dressed, head bent under the sloping roof, waiting for Madame and Monsieur to leave the house with the children in tow. Then he goes downstairs, pulls up one of the empty chairs in the dining room and, as he chews his breakfast, tries to decipher the notes Madame has left on his plate. Most of the time there is something like: Washing utensils are in the basement at the back on the right; or: Please iron the underwear too; or: Could you make a courgette-flower omelette for tonight? There are fresh courgette flowers in the vegetable compartment. Madame's handwriting is small, round and not always legible. If Viktor cannot make it out, he leaves the note to ask Lionel for clarification in the afternoon, who then reads the instructions without enthusiasm, but correctly. On Tuesdays, Viktor cleans all the bathrooms, after clearing the breakfast table and making beds, polishing the Moroccan tiles with a small blue cloth that Madame leaves out the night before.

On Wednesday mornings, Maud and Lionel are picked up by a tiny lady in an elegant suit, who is hurriedly dragged into the house by the children, as if to make sure she does not fall into the clutches of the giant thug in the doorway. She places her small ringed hand in Viktor's great man's hand and introduces herself as Maïe. I'm the *grande-maman* here, she says, beaming at Viktor, with her twinkling eyes rimmed with blue eyeliner.

On Thursdays, he tackles the house's integrated vacuum system. When he finally finds the right wall socket, he only has half an hour left for all three floors, then prepares a mountain of manges-touts for dinner and picks up the children from school. Every day they walk through the woods in front of him, every day they only turn round to look at him if it can't be helped, for example when he has to enter his number code into the keypad by the steel gate, because Lionel has forgotten his own. Viktor never forgets his code, nor his combat boots. However, he does not find Julija in front of the school gate. Is her au pair year over and she is already on her way back to Ukraine? Or deeper into Western Europe, to study in Toulouse, with her wavy matted hair, without sparing a thought for the funny German Ukrainian whom she met on the last day of that section of her life now left behind her? He could ask the little chatterbox with the curls who was with her. But no matter how hard he keeps look out in the afternoons in front of the school gate, the little one always seems to have been picked up.

August sweeps over the roof shingles of the house in the form of various hot south winds. Viktor's French is getting better. In the *Nouvel Observateur*, which Monsieur deposits in the living room, he deciphers a report about a massive sandstorm on the southern edge of the Sahara. Favoured by northerly wind currents in the Pyrenees, a layer of fine Saharan sand had been detected in the sky over France. The concentration of particulate matter reached its maximum of around 80 micrograms per cubic metre on 30 August, before the sand had silently trickled over regions of Languedoc-Roussillon, Midi-Pyrénées, Aquitaine and PACA regions, where its alkaline properties had counteracted the acid rain over the vineyards of Courbières and left minor insurance damage on the paint of the mopeds in Marseilles. That is all Viktor learns of the outside world.

And otherwise? Artichoke ratatouille with almond roast potatoes, courgette gratin with goat's cheese and fennel seeds, tabbouleh des Pieds-Noirs. When his head is swirling with new vocabulary, he swims laps in the pool behind the terrace or stands in the hallway and listens. Sometimes he thinks he hears steps. Then he opens all the doors so he can see everywhere. Sometimes the steel gate stands wide open without him having done anything. Sometimes the bell rings in Madame's practice, even though Madame is already busy with a patient. Sometimes Maud suddenly appears next to him and looks up at him, then turns on her heel and disappears round the next immaculately plastered corner. Lionel's door remains closed. Sometimes he hears the thud of music. Sometimes everything is too quiet. Once when Viktor presses his ear to the door to find out if the ten-year-old, for whose welfare he is after all responsible, is still alive, Maud suddenly appears next to him, her face smeared with biscuit and laughs as if she has caught him spying.

The weeks flash past. A dense blonde stubble sprouts on his head, which he lets grow. As his hair gets longer, the days become imperceptibly shorter.

In the dark kitchen the dishwasher purrs, the leftovers of the sage lasagne from this Friday's dinner are in a Tupperware in the fridge. From Lionel's room come the thud of a muffled bass. From Maud's room he can hear Madame's monotonous reading voice. Viktor stands at the open window of his room and looks down over the roof tiles at Monsieur, who does laps of crawl in the pool with slow, full-strength strokes. The underwater lights have been turned off; his body barely stands out against the liquid black around him. The twilight swallows the characteristic Provencal pink of the wall behind the pine trees, but the sky above glows in a three-dimensional blue that reminds Viktor of a snowball fight with Ruth and her mother that ended in tears, but that must have been in another life. The house next door is in darkness too, no light in any of the windows. When the whistle sounds, Monsieur pauses mid-stroke and briefly raises his head before pushing off from the edge of the pool. In the middle of the courtyard Julija lowers her hand.

Where did you come from? asks Viktor, coming downstairs. Visible neither from the pool nor from the room, she sits on the sloping ramp to the garage, her arms crossed behind her head, her foot loosely resting on her bare leg. In front of her, the polished surface of the motorcycle shimmers in the darkness of the garage. Julija laughs at Viktor and holds out a cigarette for him. I'm not the only one, she says in Ukrainian, who goes in and out of your house.

Her appearance fills Viktor with a sense of relief in a way that makes it impossible for him not to kiss her red mouth. Cigarette between middle and index finger, Julija puts her hand on the back of his head and kisses him back, as if there had never been any other form of greeting. She tastes of smoke and sweet apples, this could go on for ever. When she pulls him to the ground on top of her, her mouth shines wet and dark red. Viktor kisses the gap in her teeth and pushes her dress up. Her breasts are round and soft like nothing he has ever known. Her nipples stand out dark against the dusk. When his penis pushes into her, Julija grabs his upper arms, pulls herself up on him and tugs him deeper inside. Sharp stones dig into his palms and knees, he doesn't care. In Julija it is narrow and strange, and with each push, the garage entrance, the white gravel courtyard and the vaulted sky above their houses converge and expand into the immeasurable.

Didn't notice anything then? she asks later, turning her head towards Viktor. They lie side by side on their backs, their bare legs knotted together, breathing cigarette smoke into the night. Cool basement air comes out of the open garage, but the concrete under their bodies has stored the late summer warmth. The old guy, she adds, who goes in and out of your place?

She throws her head backwards and rolls her eyes. Her neck stands out pale and narrow against the ground, her shadowy hair swallows the residual light of the dusk. Monsieur has already banned him several times, she explains, and passes the cigarette over to Viktor. He has given everyone but the little one their own code, including Lionel. But it doesn't help, says Julija, and sighs quietly into the dark.

Viktor is barely listening. He lies on his back next to Julija, cool air passing over his damp penis. He has his eyes closed and looks inside himself. In his head the cornfields are waving behind his parents' new-build block. Julija rests her head in her hand and brings her mouth close to Viktor's ear. His name is Jim, she says. Used to be a mechanic.

And you, murmurs Viktor in Ukrainian. Can you pick any lock?

Oh no, says Julija, getting up and wiping a smear of spunk from her thigh. Then she turns around, walks towards the hedge next to the garage, as if this were the most normal departure in the world, and disappears the very next moment. Viktor had not noticed the gap in the greenery. For a while he stays there, squatting on his haunches in front of the open garage, finishing the cigarette and listening to Julija's steps cross next door's lawn.

Then he, too, gets up and dresses. It is already late. So as not to be seen, he makes his way through the garage. Everything in the house is quiet. In front of the door to Lionel's room, Viktor steps in something wet. Surprised, he stops in front of the small puddle. The faint glow of the night light on the skirting board is reflected in it.

‡

I stand barefoot in Jim's parlour. The floorboards are warm from the summer. They creak. Jim walks backwards and forwards, his huge fists thrust in his pockets. He shakes his head.

I'm old, he says. I can't take care of you.

Jim is our neighbour. He does not have much hair left. But hands like shovels. The veins on his arms stand out like ropes. When I press one, it rolls to the side. I'm not pressing it now. Jim walks up and down. Up and down so that that the floorboards creak.

A medal hangs on the wall of his parlour. A Cross of Lorraine. Two bars across a third one. Looks like a sword that is too short. It hangs on a small ribbon, in a wooden frame. Jim finally stops and lifts it out. He places it in my hands. The metal is heavy in my fingers. There's something on the back,

Jim explains it to me. Something about serving the fatherland and a victory, but I don't care. So, Jim can fight. That is enough for me.

But you are a fighter, I say.

No, says Jim. I was a fighter.

She will take care of you, says Jim.

It's not a she, I say.

What is it then? Jim asks. An insect?

A boy, I say.

Jim ponders. His head nods from side to side. He doesn't look very fierce.

Is he big?

Yes, I say.

Does he look like a fighter?

He looks like the Hulk, I say. Only without hair. Jim doesn't know any comics. He certainly doesn't know who the Hulk is.

Does he think like a fighter?

I shrug my shoulders. What does a fighter think like? I ask.

Like you, says Jim.

9

Where have you been this whole time, Maud asks the boy with the curly hair, running up the path to school between her and Julija. The kids have been back at school for two weeks already. It is just before eight, the magpies are wide awake and sitting in the pine trees in the front gardens. Overtaken by a column of cars with children in the back seats, the small group leaves the walls of the villas behind them. Viktor looks at Julija from behind. Her neck is soft and white, her black hair standing out wildly on all sides reminds him of night. She steps smoothly over the air roots at the edge of the forest, where the morning sun makes the conifers scent. Appendicitis! the curly-headed child calls melodramatically. I was in hospital, properly! *Apendytsyt,* Julija translates and turns to Viktor as she walks along. Are Madame and Monsieur beginning to trust your Nazi arse as far as they can throw you?

Nazi, phhhh, says Lionel from the side. He stamps along next to Viktor, keeping his eyes fixed the forest floor. As he does so, he blows out his cheeks slightly, as only the French know how to do. You're kind of a Russian, aren't you? Russians can't be Nazis.

Lionel, calls Julija, and gives him a friendly kick. Don't tell me you can speak Ukrainian now.

Lionel laughs silently and shakes his head. Together they enter the car park in front of the school, where the coupés stand in the morning light like koi in a pond. As the little group winds their way between the rows of parked cars in single file, Viktor grabs Lionel by the shoulders and says quietly: I know you are not afraid.

Lionel stands rooted to the spot. He looks at the children's watch on his wrist, a swatch in bright yellow like the corn-fields in Viktor's home, but he cannot know that.

No, I'm not afraid, he says, as if he has learned the phrase by heart. The watch on his wrist shows two minutes before eight as Viktor bends down to him. He sees the light flecks in Lionel's brown eyes. The white is slightly reddened, the lids swollen, as if he had been crying all night.

But I, Viktor says slowly and clearly in French, will take care of you. Lionel wants to get away, but Viktor is holding his shoulders. It's now or never he thinks and says: I promise you.

Monday. Ironing day. Piles of laundry on the dining table; in the kitchen the pumpkin quiche for that evening is already in the oven; Viktor stands at the ironing board, neck awkwardly bent over, shaking his head in disbelief as he does every week, that Madame and Monsieur like their underpants ironed, when suddenly the old man appears behind him as if from nowhere.

You're good at that, he says, looking on with interest as Viktor carries on. In his right hand a wooden walking stick, with the handle hung over his arm. A metal tip protrudes from the bottom end of the stick, which lends something military to his appearance. On his head a dark-green beret that reinforces this impression. From under the brim a few wisps of hair protrude, his lined face is covered with white beard stubble. Viktor takes him for eighty or so. Although he only reaches up to Viktor's shoulder, the old man does not seem to be impressed in the least by his stature.

Good to know you're are not a weakling, says Jim and surveys him without embarrassment.

How do you get in here?

Oof, that's not hard. I was in the air force when I was your age. Whether I'm repairing navigation systems, *mon fils*, or just popping in here . . .

Viktor must have a look of surprise on his face, Jim acknowledges it with a triumphant grin. That's all right then, he says, as if in answer to something that Viktor has not said. Jim lowers his head and turns to walk away, but Viktor holds him by the arm. But what are you doing here? he asks a little too loudly.

With a single movement of his powerful hand, the old man swipes Viktor's hand away and frees himself. Walking away he shakes his head muttering: Well, someone has to check up. Stunned, Viktor follows Jim out of the house and watches him as he crosses the yard. Someone has to! His walking stick digs into the white yard gravel. Who knows what will happen if no one keeps an eye, Jim mutters.

Keeps an eye? Viktor calls after him. Keeps an eye on what? But the old man does not seem to hear him, because the courtyard gate closes behind his wide, bent back and Viktor is left standing alone in the open doorway, with the iron still in his hand. From then on Jim seems to make no effort to keep his inspection visits secret from Viktor. Suddenly there he is standing on the terrace, in the basement, in the stairwell, nodding kindly to Viktor, before turning back to his own business. In the mornings he seems to keep out of his way, at least Viktor does not see him. Mostly Jim shows up in the afternoon, when Maud and Lionel are there; they treat him like a natural phenomenon whose movements cannot be influenced.

At one point, he is banging around loudly in Monsieur and Madame's bedroom: pulling out the drawers of the dresser, inspecting Monsieur's bedside table and leafing through picture books, as if he were looking for something—though he himself hardly knows what it is. He rips open the old wardrobe where Monsieur's suits hang, pulls out underwear and shoe boxes and throws everything behind him on the parquet floor. When Viktor storms into the room, he nods to him and simply turns the tables: Ah yes, *mon fils*, what are you doing here?

One time, Viktor finds him in Lionel's room, with Lionel sitting at his desk, bent over a piece of paper. The old man is standing directly behind the boy and has placed his huge paws on his narrow shoulders, the two are immersed in quiet conversation. When Viktor stands next to them, their murmured exchange falls silent.

The next morning Viktor interrupts the bedmaking to examine Lionel's desk, trying not to move anything out of place, nor to make any noise. The old man might be lurking in the house and catch him in the act. Nonsense, he says to himself. There are lots of bits of paper in the drawers, many of them crumpled. Lionel has drawn graffiti lettering in bright colours, dark red and neon green, three-dimensional letters that stand out. On one sheet Viktor recognizes the lettering from the day before. *Ta gueule*, he deciphers. The letters are outlined thickly with a black sharpie and look like limbs, but weirdly twisted into each other. Under the L, Lionel has drawn light-brown spots that drip from the letter like vomit.

Who is this Jim actually? Viktor asks in a studiedly casual manner. Madame is standing at the sink filling the saucepan with hot water, the remains of the Béchamel sauce foam up white. *Eh ben*, she says, and turns off the tap. Our neighbour, his grandson is also looked after by an au pair. She's been there quite a while, seems nice. You might have come across her?

Um, yes, Viktor mutters and strokes his hand over the blonde stubble on his head. This Jim, he then asks, he does not know what word to choose, is *un peu*—

Ah, you find him odd, laughs Madame and grabs the tea towel from the hook. He has a bit of grenade shrapnel in his occipital lobe, she says, pointing to the back of her head with the horn salad spoon. When he was about your age, he fought for the FFL against the Germans. Actually, the FAFL, the air force, like André Malraux—but you probably don't know him, right? Jim was a specialist for small-aircraft navigation systems, there's a Cross of Lorraine hanging in his dining room that was given to him personally by de Gaulle. He was shot down by the Nazis, says Madame, and blushes slightly, that is the Germans, over Paris. And so as not crash down onto his own people, he had executed a spectacular emergency landing in the Seine. A veteran, she says, wringing out the wet cloth. He is being seen by a colleague of mine as a private patient. Medical confidentiality, of course. The shrapnel has encapsulated decades ago and won't cause any further problems. But if he sometimes seems a little, Madame sighs and rubs her hands with a Norwegian ointment next to the sink, well, strange, that's because of this shrapnel. She looks up at him and turns to walk away. He is, *comment dire*, always very close to things. Have you noticed that?

Viktor shrugs his shoulders.

In the doorway, Madame turns back again and looks him in the face uncertainly. Why? she asks. Oh, says Viktor, no reason.

10

So don't tell me that this Jim is the grandpa of the kid you look after. Viktor is standing in Jim's living room in the neighbouring house looking at the medal above the sideboard. The cross is narrow and black, two bars, one above the other, across the longer bar on a bronze sword sheath. The plaque in his hand weighs more than he expected. *Patriam Servando Victoriam Tulit*, he deciphers on the reverse, but what's it got to do with him, Viktor, anyway?

Don't stand about being annoying, Julija moans, just help me instead. She is standing on a ladder, scrubbing the wall with a natural sponge. It is the last one that evening, the other three living-room walls still bear traces of damp. The walls of Benjamin's room, which he had decorated with crayons, are already dry, but she still has to get a lime tart into the oven ready for tomorrow. Today is Friday, her host parents are at the cinema, as every week, the little one is fast asleep, the heavy tread of Viktor's combat boots creaks on the boards. Stop, she says, and hands him down the water. What a guy, she thinks, but he is scared when faced with a confused old *Did* like Jim.

Viktor strokes his hand over the stubble on his head, shakes off the unpleasant feeling that has crept up on him and takes the bucket from Julija's hand. Her legs emerge smooth and white from her cut-off jeans. She is standing on the ladder, stretching up reach a grey spot on the wall at the top right. Viktor turns away so as not to stare, places the bucket on the floor and rips the windows open. The cool evening air floods in and dissipates the smell of the dirty water. When he closes the wooden shutters, blocking out the light of the streetlamp in front of the house, a warm darkness settles over them both.

You don't really like enclosed spaces, says Julija and wraps her arms around his hips from behind, do you? Without a sound she has climbed down from the ladder and moved in close behind him. Viktor feels her soft breasts pressing into his back. For a moment he considers telling her about the locked bedroom door at home, his pleas, his shit in the lunch box in his school bag, but then the darkness has also settled over that. They move off a little, staring steadily into each other's eyes as they strip off combat boots, socks and trousers and drop them on the floor. Whoever looks away first, will be overwhelmed with fear and shame, but neither of them looks away. They still have their eyes locked as Julija perches on the windowsill and wraps her legs around Viktor's hips. His penis slips into her, hard and smooth, and pulses in the damp walls of this strange space, above which an infinite number of suns explode. When Julija groans as he thrusts into her for the last time, Viktor hears Jim's heavy steps entering the kitchen. Jim murmurs to himself: *Mais qu'est-ce que j'en fais alors?* I can't protect him. *Je ne peux pas.*

11

A magpie sits on the wall to the street. Under the light of the streetlamp, the bright spots of its plumage stand out from the darkness all around. Viktor is sat with his legs hanging over the windowsill smoking one of Julija's cigarettes, his bare feet resting on the cool roof shingles. Noiselessly the steel gate in front of him opens, Monsieur drives in over the raked gravel of the yard, which flickers like the TV screen in the moonlight. When he takes off his helmet and throws his head back, Viktor raises his hand to say hello, but Monsieur does not seem to notice him.

It is almost one. Viktor stubs out the cigarette and climbs back into his room. He flops backwards onto the bed. Tomorrow is his day off. At last he will empty his backpack with the crane emblem, which has been standing open in the middle of the floor since his arrival months ago. Finally. He will throw his clothes into the wooden chest. And call Matusja. Or maybe he will leave all that and take the bus into Marseilles, see the Mediterranean. Maybe Julija will come with him. The Mediterranean, the harbour, the magpies, Julija. That is the last thing Viktor thinks. As Monsieur, who has pulled off his motorcycle leathers in the garage, quietly climbs up the stairs and presses down the doorhandle to Lionel's room, Viktor is oblivious.

Breakfast! Maud is standing at the head of his bed, looking at him with interest as he wakes up. You still have your trousers on from yesterday, she notes. Do you always sleep like that? Viktor starts awake and looks around. The clouds chase across the rectangular morning sky of the window. The bedspread under him is still there just as he laid it out the previous morning, he is dressed in jeans and T-shirt lying on top. The travel alarm clock on his bedside table says ten past eight. What about my day off? Breakfast! calls Maud again. We are going on a trip, and you should come too!

Bien sûr, says Monsieur and smiles softly. He leans back on the dining chair and silently stirs his espresso. We explained the day you arrived, my wife and I.

But he didn't understand a word back then, Maud splutters with a mouth full of cornflakes, and even Viktor just does not understand that but he nods anyway, just in case. Maud smiles and snuggles in under Monsieur's arm, keeping an eye on Viktor. Lionel is silent, stuffs the cornflakes into his mouth and seems not to be there at all.

Madame winks and sips her coffee. Our wonderful au pair has learned French better than anyone would have thought possible on his somewhat surprising arrival, she says. Victoire, Madame passes Viktor a china bowl with rock-hard piece of bread, Lionel turned ten years old just before you arrived. Since we didn't have time to celebrate—because you came along and caused so much trouble—because we couldn't celebrate, we thought we would drive out to our holiday home on the coast. It's barely three-quarters of an hour's drive away. From there we will take a short hike into the Calanques, you have certainly heard of them, haven't you? You had no other plans, did you? says Madame as clearly as the voice of the trainer on a language-learning CD. *Est ce-que tu me comprends?*

After he has cleared the breakfast table with Madame and listened to her dispense some tips about smart housekeeping (we don't think its right to throw away old bread—that gives the children a false impression of running a household—but if you, Victoire, had dipped your baguette in your coffee, it would have been soft. But in East Germany this is not usual, am I right?), he quickly ducks into one of bathrooms (but please hurry, Victoire, you don't want to be the last one out), grabs the backpack of the East Elbe District Transport Company (perfect that you are already done, Victoire, my husband may need your help) and then goes down into the yard.

Monsieur is leaning against the wall of the house in front of the fully packed boot of the Lexus and stubs his cigarette into a silver can, which immediately disappears into his shirt pocket. Except for him, no one is out yet, but now Viktor cannot go back inside. He leans against the wall alongside him.

They stand like this for a while. Monsieur, head leant back, follows the flights of magpies through his mirrored sunglasses. Viktor blinks across the snow-white gravel. This would be the moment for a conversation between men, rather between a man and a boy on his way to becoming a man. But Monsieur is busy with the magpies. Only as Madame comes out of the house with the children, does he turn his head to one side, smile just past Viktor and say gently: You don't have any shoes on yet, Victoire.

They drive a short distance along the Autoroute du Sud, leaving behind Montagne Sainte-Victoire (it has your name, Victoire, look!), which rises above the city like a broken tooth, along with the hustle and bustle of the Marseilles highway. Just before the exit, they are overtaken by a group of laughing young men who shout through the open windows, offering to buy the car, but Monsieur shakes his head with a smile and Madame quickly winds up the windows. They turn into a country road and then into a smaller country road, lined with a string of picturesque villages, like in a Provence guide, all of which they leave behind. At an immaculately manicured roundabout, a large light-brown snake lies in the sun; Madame roars past in the Lexus so close that Viktor turns his head to make sure the snake is not reduced to mush. Monsieur chats with Madame in muted tones until the breaks between sentences grow longer and longer. And then no one speaks any more.

Lionel sits in the back, headphones on and eyes closed, Maud is perched on her child seat observing Viktor as he tries not to think of Julija, looking instead at the passing landscape. The cypresses swirl in the wind. Slanting light knots the sky.

The holiday house comes into view at the end of a grove of trees. It looks like the cube in this dazzling cardboard book that his half-sister once gave him before she started seeing that bastard. The Magic Cube. Imagine a cube. What does this cube look like? What material is it made of? How far is the cube from the ground?

It is a snow-white box with a glazed rear wall that looks out over a gently sloping lavender field. Beyond the lavender, the world seems to come to an end.

They set off in the early afternoon. A gently ascending path leads through the middle of the lavender. Viktor has tied his combat boots to his East Elbe District Transport Company rucksack, he feels them bouncing behind his back and ignores Monsieur's smile and Madame's remark, that he should be careful not to hurt his feet, they don't want to have to cut short the hike (not on account of a strapping outdoor lad like him, right?). It is his day off, after all; officially at least. The well-trodden earth under his feet feels warm and dry, and Viktor thinks of the holidays with his parents on the Polish coast of the Baltic Sea. He remembers walking the perfectly straight path through a summery corner of forest to Łeba, to see the huge creeping sand dune Łącka Góra. Walking along with hundreds of other holiday makers on foot or on rental bikes, now and again being overtaken by charabancs full of older people, all craning forward, because they know, like everyone else, what they are going to see but never exactly what it will look like. Will its surface be covered with hatching like the Baltic Sea or will it be as smooth as a fried egg in a pan? Will it glow yellow or have the colour of the pierogi the holiday makers will eat that evening? And above all, what part of the forest will it have swallowed again under a mass of sand since they were last there? Matusja had always prepared blood sausage, bread and boiled eggs, which they never ate, because halfway to the dune there was a clearing with three food stalls. Viktor runs through the French lavender and thinks of the bread and dripping his father had bought him every time despite Matusja's protests. He walks through the lavender and thinks of the huge jars on the counters of the snack stalls, with mustard cucumbers like rare marine animals. It seems to him that it was decades ago that he saw the gherkin jars, the day trippers, the forest and the wandering dune, because at the moment he is marching through a lavender field, from the depths of which come strange sounds that he cannot identify. Viktor stops and turns his shaved head into the south wind. He imagines agricultural equipment left behind abandoned in the middle of the fields, the engines left running for decades, until someone finds them and pulls out the ignition key. But Madame catches up with him and brings him back to reality when she stops behind him and explains, in the most beautiful travel-guide French, that these are crickets, their lovely chirping (beautiful, right, Victoire? We hear them into late September) is an emblem of Provence.

Maud and Lionel are far ahead of him. Lionel has a long branch in his hand and is knocking the heads off the cornflowers at the edge of the field. Maud runs along beside him and stops from time to time to squat down and observe something. Every now and then she puts something in her pocket before jumping up again and catching up with Lionel. Viktor walks ten metres behind the children; Monsieur and Madame walk further back, talking in subdued tones and in rapid French full of difficult constructions; he thinks he catches terms such as insurance, performance and customer loyalty, which he remembers from the intensive course he did, the unit on *Travailler en France: Vocabulaire professional*, and does not even try to follow the conversation. The hot late summer's day makes him sleepy, and Viktor for once does not even think about Julija. He walks through a flowering lavender field, as if it were a field of poppies, and thinks of nothing. As the bright rocky cliff of the coast rises in front of them, he sees Maud and Lionel crawling halfway up between the cacti.

The path over the rocks is so narrow that you can only walk in single file. But they have hardly reached the cliff when someone up in the windswept sky must have pressed a switch, because all at once the family is hardly recognizable. Joking and laughing, they scramble along the path, constantly overtaking one another, constantly jostling, talking over one another; Maud squealing with pleasure when the spray splashes so high that she gets wet. In the roar of the surf they toss phrases back and forth like shuttles that are carried away by the wind; they lean into it, so their jackets inflate behind them. Monsieur runs his hand through Lionel's hair before grabbing him and swirling him around. Lionel fights back, punching about him wildly, and for the length of a gust of wind, he really looks like a boy who has just turned ten. Maud is sitting on Monsieur's shoulders, she spreads out her short arms and calls: Papa is the fastest, Papa is the TGV! And Madame jumps back and forth snapping one photo after another. Suddenly this is how it is and it goes on and on. Once developed, the film will show that it wasn't just the family laughing. Viktor too will wear on his face the expression of incredulous, uncertain laughter of an almost adult. In one of the pictures he will discover Lionel, standing on a rock in the dazzling coastal light, looking straight out of the picture, as if to call out to him: Stay with us, don't leave! He will clearly remember that Lionel had called something completely different. But that's how it will seem to him anyway.

Far below them, turquoise water cuts mini-fjords into the rock. Hard to believe, how the spray is flung up high as a house before plunging back into the water. Hard to believe, how the sailboats stand motionless in the water, or does it just look like that? Between the limestone rocks strange plants grow as big as Maud. In between them lichens cling to the rock, Viktor has never seen anything like them before. When he reaches out to take hold of a fleshy giant, Madame shouts against the wind: Don't touch, it's poisonous! Too late— Viktor will spend another week finding fine white barbs under the skin of his palms, which will remind him of that day.

All the while, Maud has been emptying the contents of her trouser pockets into the spray, piece by piece, with outstretched arms. Every time a shot disappears into the surf, she cheers. Madame calls out not to go so close to the edge as Maud turns to her and shouts: I'm making mussels! Madame stows the camera in the case and brings out thermos flasks and madeleines from her backpack for the picnic on the cliff; she has a nervous twitch in the right eyelid that irritates her. Monsieur sits a little off to the side near an agave and telephones against the wind, it seems to be something to do with work. Either they haven't seen that the pellets in Maud's hand are vineyard snails, or they don't care. It doesn't matter, Viktor thinks. Some lighter, some darker, some with red stripes on the shells. Some crack on impact, some roll into crevasses, some land in the sea. Viktor is just about to go over, but Lionel has already put his arm round Maud.

Maud, they don't turn into mussels.

But when I throw them into the sea they learn to swim.

No, these are snails that can't learn to swim.

Mais si!

No, they just die.

What?

They snuff it, your snails.

You're mad!

That's enough, says Lionel quite calmly. Tonight, he'll come to you.

The next moment, Lionel has lifted his sister up and is swirling her in a circle, just as Monsieur had done with him. Tonight, he sings a small, mean song, tonight you will get the visit! And with a trembling chin, Maud flies through the gusts of wind and shouts: *Maman*! Madame actually looks up from her picnic preparations. *Maman*! But she sees nothing. She doesn't see what Viktor sees. Tonight, Lionel sings and grins, tonight! And instead of rushing and scooping up her children firmly in both arms, she fumbles the camera out of the case to snap this strange turning movement. *Maman*! Madame tries to ignore the twitching in her eye and clicks the button at the very moment when Lionel looks at her briefly mid-spin. Tonight, tonight . . . , Lionel sings. But Madame does not hear anything either. Only Viktor hears, as Lionel sings into the wind, as if he were singing for himself: . . . he'll fuck you to the moon and back. Then he has already turned away, and Lionel, with the howling Maud in his arms, carries on turning.

Back in the cottage Viktor heads towards the kitchen and, with Madame's help, prepares the first sea mussels of his life. He steams red onions in oil, adds garlic, takes a bouquet of dried thyme from the large jar directly above the stove and crumbles it into the pan, while Madame brings the mussels to the boil. One by one, they open and make little sounds. She lifts the ones that stay shut out of the pot and drops them into the sink, where they make clapping sounds like the vineyard snails on the rocks, but this time it is Viktor who is elsewhere. He stands next to Madame in silence, as she gives a running commentary on what they are doing, trying to concentrate on the kilo of freshly washed tomatoes in front of his nose, which he cuts into fine cubes and adds to the onions. When Madame pours some of the mussel juice into the pan, a smell of seaweed and sea salt spreads through the kitchen, as if they were still standing on the Calanques.

They eat out on the terrace. The mussel shells are the same colour as the sky that arcs above them. The family scoops them out with small silver spoons, Viktor tries to copy them. Next to the porcelain tureen with the mussels stands a second tureen for the shells. Viktor sees it filling up as they spoon out their supper, and at least Madame and Monsieur joke and eat, and the crickets creak in all four directions. Lionel still smiles his fine, mean smile and talks more than in the whole of last week. Monsieur laughs at his jokes: What is spooky and you eat it on the beach? Sand witches!

Only Maud is silent and pushes her plate away after the fifth or sixth mussel. And Viktor, who already lost his appetite at the sound of the shells opening in the saucepan and has been chewing on his not-quite-fresh white bread the whole time, at some point reaches down beside him and pulls Maud onto his lap. She does not struggle, leans her light back against his chest and lets her arms hang down limply. Again, Viktor hears the sound of the shell cracking on the rock, hears the crickets around them, and hears Lionel telling a joke he does not understand. Carefully, so as not to crush her, he puts his arms around Maud's belly.

When the family has finished eating, someone presses the switch for the second time that day. Piles of blue-black shells lie scattered across the table. Imperceptibly, Lionel closes back inside himself until he sits motionless and bent at the table with his hands in his lap. On Viktor's lap Maud's legs twitch a few times in her sleep. Monsieur, arms folded in front of his narrow chest, looks out into the night. Only Madame and Viktor on the night-time terrace look around, quiet and astonished— each in their own world. It shoots through Viktor's head: Can it really be that she did not hear Lionel earlier? That cannot be true, thinks Madame, and feels the twitching in her eyelid again, it can't be true, what she heard Lionel singing earlier. The wind has dropped for today, no one speaks.

‡

Don't cry, says Lionel.

We are in the weekend house. My brother and I are sharing our room with the au pair. The au pair is sitting behind the house, listening to the ocean. I bet he is just thinking about his girlfriend. She is an au pair too. But a girl. Maybe they're even called au pairs because they always want to be in pairs.

His backpack lies on the bed by the window. Lionel and I have the bunk bed against the wall. Lionel is on top. His bare foot swaying over the edge of the bed. He'll fall off if he's not careful, I think.

Stop crying. It was just a joke.

I pull my knees up to my chin. Pebbles and snail shells spill out of my trouser pockets They are black as night. I arrange them on my pillow. One snail shell is heavy because there is still something inside. I feel inside with my finger. Feels like slime. When you throw slime at the window, it slides down slowly.

Papa would never do that with you, says Lionel.

What does Papa do?

None of your business.

But.

No way.

After all, I am his child, I say, and wrinkle my nose noisily.
And?

You're not! I exclaim in triumph.

Lionel says: Exactly.

I want Papa to do with me what he does with Lionel. I won't say it. But I wish for it with all my strength. I wouldn't cry like Lionel.

I throw a snail at the window. Hard as I can. It pops. Lionel's foot is still now. I throw another one. Hard as I can. It cracks. Another. Hard as I can. I count the snails in flight. Gradually it's turning into a game. With the fourth, the window breaks. Probably a stone. With the fifth the glass splinters. The splinters fall onto the au pair's bed. At the sixth snail Lionel jumps off his bed. The seventh snail shoots through the air. Lionel throws himself on top of me. Hard as he can.

He presses my fists into the mattress and looks like the Hulk. Just not so green. I giggle without meaning to. Lionel bends over and hisses into my ear: Stop now.

But I can't. The incredible Hulk is sitting on my chest. For a moment I hear the ocean roar. Then he drops a glob of spit. It's white like foam. It lands in my mouth.

That's what Papa does to me, says Lionel. That!

In the middle of the night, the au pair climbs in through the window. He cuts himself on the shards on his bed. He curses softly in his own language.

12

You're quiet today, Victoire? cries Madame, who is hovering by the front door. Viktor has not said much since they've been back, and this Monday morning not a single word.

Viktor is busy studying Madame's notes on the domestic tasks for the week just begun while soaking a chunk of left-over baguette scratched with butter in his bowl of coffee. Madame blinks nervously, waiting for Viktor's answer, which does not come; then she is out of the house. Viktor listens to the noise of the car engine as she rolls through the steel gate on her way to make a home visit. He is alone with his thoughts, the uncleared breakfast table, the unmade beds, the unironed laundry in the cellar, the fish soup for the evening. He has until just before four, after that he has to fetch the children. Everything is fine, says Viktor in his father's language and tackles the mountain of ironing in the laundry cellar. That sounds reassuring, so he says it again: everything is fine.

I don't understand any German, but it seems like an occupational hazard of au pair existence that we all talk to ourselves, he suddenly hears right behind him. Viktor spins round. Julija is standing at the entrance to the garage and lifts her arms towards him with a laugh. Her shock of hair stands out like a paper cut against the incoming morning light. Oh no, *pardon*: I didn't want to startle you. She strolls down the ramp and looks around curiously. Her gaze wanders over bicycles under covers, metal shelves, a freezer, a wine rack fixed to the wall opposite a homeopathic home pharmacy with meticulously labelled compartments, next to the cleaning utensils: three mops of different types and colours, four matching buckets and, hanging on a large hook, the hose of the in-house suction system. In the half-light of a side room are the washing machine and dryer. Julija moves just behind Viktor, who is working on one of Monsieur's shirts with the iron. As she presses against him, Viktor feels her breasts. With her flat hand she gropes for his chest. You have goosebumps, she says matter-of-factly. Does that have anything to do with me?

Viktor shrugs. With a hiss the steam from the iron rises in a cloud in front of him. She detaches herself and looks at him from the side. Everything okay with you? she asks. *Vse po poryadku?*

Yes, of course, says Viktor. *Vse po poryadku.*

You're still thinking about the old guy.

Viktor is silent. In front of him the steam rises from the iron. He breathes deeply but the air does not reach him, it never does and never enough, although it flows in with Julija through the open garage door. Julija looks around curiously until Viktor finally turns off the iron and follows her up into the house.

They pass through the rooms in silence as if they were looking for something, without knowing what it was: she in worn out sneakers, he with bare feet on the tiles. Julija stops briefly in front of Lionel's brand-new collection of pens strewn across his bed, strokes over the smoothed sheets, then strolls on. Viktor, his lungs knotted in his chest, follows her silently. He could go to the kitchen with Julija and let her taste the fish soup, which stands ready on the ceramic hob. He could tell her what's going on in his head. But he lets it drop. They cross the living room. Julija's hands drift over the ledge on the chimney breast, knock on the wooden stack next to it. Finally she stops in front of a narrow door. What's in there? she asks and turns the handle.

Inside the tiny room is a built-in hi-fi system with a record player, CD player, two tape decks, a receiver and shiny black knobs for fine tuning. Shelves of Monsieur's music collection line the wall up to the ceiling like an unearthed treasure. Julija pulls the door behind her and looks at Viktor in the faint light. Her eyebrows are bushy above her searching gaze. Viktor breaks out in a sweat. Open it, he says.

Julija just shakes her head and pulls a record off the shelf. She lifts the lid and places it on the turntable. LED lights light up, the disc begins to turn; carefully Julija places the needle in the groove. Do you know this one? she asks. She turns up the volume; from ten speakers, through the closed door, they hear it spread across the house, the kitchen, living room, dining room and terrace: Udo Lindenberg and the Panic Orchestra. Fucking shit. Viktor opens the door, gasping for air. Oh, come on, Julija shouts after him, trying to make herself heard above the volume. You don't like Udo Lindenberg? You are German!

Lefty scum, Viktor curses in his head and says out loud: I listen to different German stuff.

What? calls Julija. The music is so loud, I can't understand you.

Different Germans, he repeats. Steel Thunderstorm, Stuka . . .

He pushes Julija aside and turns the sound down until Udo is muttering from the loudspeakers at a tolerable volume. When he turns away to finally get out of the little room, Julija puts her hand in his and smiles. She smells a little of sweat.

Ah all that Nazi stuff of yours, she says, uncovering the gap between her front teeth. Do your lot have to listen to it?

He would prefer not to listen to anything now; just to fuck her, right here in the door frame. At this moment he cannot stand her.

Julija turns to the record shelf and lets the fingers of her free hand slide over the covers before she pulls out the new Iggy Pop album. Iggy on the cover has the same facial expression as Viktor, only his hair is long and straggles down to his shoulders. She skilfully turns the knob down again until Udo fades away. *And she's already gone, And she's* already *gone*, the last repetition is no longer to be heard. Blood rushes into Viktor's ears.

This Jim, he says, just before the air runs out. Without loosening her grip, Julija one-handedly changes the record on the turntable, which begins to rotate, slowly at first, then faster. She places the diamond stylus in the groove, and Viktor takes a breath: So, your *Did*—

Forget him, Julija interrupts. She lifts the needle again and puts it down just before the second song. The guitar starts, and Julija lets her head fall back. Her hand still in his, she rocks her slender body to the intro, quietly, framed by Monsieur's record collection on the shelves. Iggy Pop sings: *I want to fuck her on the floor, among my books of ancient lore,* and she says: After all it doesn't bother anyone if he walks about in your house.

Does he do the same in other houses?

Only yours, I think.

And what did he lose here?

Nothing, says Julija and sings along to the chorus with her Ukrainian accent: *I gotta Nazi girlfriend.* He is just a protector, our *Did.*

Protector? Viktor wants to hiss back: He should be locked away. He is incapable of shaking off Julija's hand—why is she doing this? The walls of the room close in on him with a sudden lurch, and he feels that pressure behind his eyes, the switch in his brain that he has almost forgotten in the madness of the last months. Lock 'em up and let them bleed, he thinks. First smash into the soft tissues, and then lock them up until there is nothing left. Out loud he says: Got to get some fresh air, and pushes out of the room, dragging Julija with him.

In the yard, she winds her hand out of his fist. For a moment it is quite unclear who is holding whom. Viktor stands in front of Julija and sucks the air into his lungs. Breathing is a good thing, he thinks, a good thing. His chest is rising and falling as if they have had sex.

You sure, she asks carefully, that everything is okay?

Viktor nods. With his eyes, he searches out the opening in the hedge. Julija walks over the gravel gently and pulls the branches apart. Shall we see each other at school, *Nazi boyfriend*? she asks, as she slips smoothly into the green. Of course, Viktor murmurs into the clear air of the yard, no problem.

He hears her sneakers disappearing behind the hedge. *It's not her baby-fine blonde hair, it's more the desert in her stare*, booms Iggy Pop from the house. His voice mixes with the crunching of the gravel underfoot as Viktor walks back inside.

Later at school, he makes his way through the fathers in their polo shirts, climbs awkwardly over badminton rackets and golf caddies, steps on one mother's toes, wipes the sweat from the bridge of his nose, jumps out of the way of a group of sixth-graders on skateboards, turns from side to side, fights down his racing heartbeat, and discovers Maud, who it seems has been trotting after him for a while, then finally finds Lionel in front of the entrance to the school library. As always, he looks past Viktor. Next to him sits Benjamin, the little boy with glasses from next door. And beside him Julija, the gap in her teeth quite visible now. Do you know the story of the hare and the hedgehog? she is asking in French as he drops down next to her out of breath. Yes, do you know it? Benjamin repeats, but Viktor does not understand the words *lapin* and *hérisson*. Breathe, he thinks, nice and steady, in and out. It is as if everything is clearly laid out before his eyes, but he just cannot piece it all together yet. Only on the way back through the woods, when Julija puts her narrow hand on his back, does he start to catch his breath again. His shirt is drenched with sweat, but Julija just lets her hand rest on it while she laughs with Benjamin and Maud about something.

‡

We are back, and everything is back to normal. Day and night. Okay, nothing is normal.

Morning all, says Jim stumbling down the stairs.

We are eating breakfast. Maman starts. Papa opens his mouth. Then he shuts it again. The au pair's bread hangs in mid-air. Lionel stares into his cocoa.

With my mouth full I shout: Good morning, Jim! My bread and jam falls into my cup. Cocoa splashes out over the table. Nobody says anything.

Jim nods kindly to me and yawns. Just passing, he grabs Papa's coffee. Papa opens his mouth to protest. But Jim gulps it down in one go. Coffee drips from his unshaven chin. Papa closes his mouth again.

Where have you been? Maman asks.

In Lionel's room, says Jim.

She smiles, bewildered.

Checking everything is in order, Jim adds and rests his huge hand on the shoulder of the au pair. The ropes on his arm are steel blue. The au pair draws his shaved head in. It doesn't look very fierce.

It's actually your job, says Jim kindly. Then he turns around and leaves the house.

Through the open patio door, we hear him shuffling away. Then we hear only the magpies.

Papa pours himself another coffee. Maman rubs her little eyes. Lionel is still staring into his cocoa. There really is only cocoa in it. The bread and jam float on top. I fish it out and stuff it in my mouth. One half stays inside, the other dribbles out. Cocoa runs down my neck and onto my T-shirt. Still no one tells me off.

The au pair looks at each of us in turn.

Jim is slowly becoming senile, says Papa.

What does senile mean? I ask.

Papa says he has a screw loose. A screw loose? asks the au pair. Oh man. He really doesn't have a clue.

13

The autumn chases greedy magpies across the front gardens. They break their necks on the patio door and lie by the pool until Viktor scoops them up and throws them into the bin. It seems to him that he has been here for ever. As he makes his way through the daily to-do list, he thinks of Julija. Julija, and her crazy smile. Julija, and the way she ignores him when it comes to the old man. Does she have no protective instinct? While his thoughts wander to her nipples, he tries out phrases he has fished out of the froth of the passing days: *je m'en vais* (Julija), *je me suis régalé, merci* (Monsieur), *Pieds-Noir* (Maïe), *grenouille* (Maud), *tu me fais chier* (Lionel). But mostly he thinks in his and Julija's mother tongue. Just finish this ironing, I have two hours left. Then the white wine sauce for tonight. How long have I been here now, hold on, so I arrived on 23rd of June; today is 28th of October, so that's 127 days, divided by seven makes what? Eighteen weeks and two days, almost five months, that is already two whole seasons, not bad, mate, not bad. Everything is fine.

Sometimes he does a lap of the pool. The surface of the water vibrates with the bass coming from the loudspeakers built into the pool walls. Viktor puts all the other speakers in the house and on the terrace on mute, so he only hears the music when he goes under. Then Iggy Pop's sexy chorus about the Nazi girlfriend envelops him. He did not bother changing the record, and Iggy Pop reminds him of Julija. With powerful strokes, he parts the film of dust on the surface of the water, blown over from the courtyard by the cool wind. Later, sitting shivering on the terrace, he dries off in the pale sun, and thinks of Julija again. Actually, he thinks about her all the time. Viktor thinks about Julija, so that he does not have to think about anything else.

On some days, he walks slowly up the quiet forest path to the École du Forêt and looks up at the slanted light in the tops of the trees. But mostly he has to run. Julija is always there ahead of him, with Lionel and Maud waiting next to her. Once Lionel shows her his oversized folder full of expensive felt pens. Julija borrows a few. In case I get some free time, she says, then I will do a drawing and show you later.

Viktor only gets to think properly when he is alone, and that is rare. Twice a week, a wiry Moroccan comes by with gold crowns on his canines; he looks after the gardens in the whole neighbourhood. In pristine overalls he strolls through the garden and adjusts the lawn sprinkler between the pine trees. On Tuesdays, the *femme de ménage* comes to dust the bookshelves and clean the windows. Occasionally, she drags Viktor along with her into the city for errands and tells him about her life as a single mother, so that Madame shakes her head in the evening, when Viktor suddenly starts speaking in a broad Marseilles dialect. Maïe also never misses a Wednesday without paying a visit to Maud and Lionel, as she puts it. She sits in the shade of the living-room blinds and has Viktor brew up an espresso before fetching the children from their rooms and chauffeuring them either to dance lessons (Maud), to motor-cross (Lionel) or to the children's opera in Marseilles (both of them). Every time she says goodbye and he helps her into her jacket, she turns to Viktor and says that he should, *s'il-te-plait*, think of himself as her third grandchild; she has always wanted a strapping lad like him in the family. Once she brings a notebook for him. It is bound in soft leather, the pages with pale-green lines and yellowed at the edges; the book seems to have been in her possession for several decades. As she hands it to him, she gives Viktor's fingertips a squeeze and says that he should write his new vocabulary in there, and if he likes, she can sometimes listen to him go through them, if her schedule permits, because she probably understands enough German and wouldn't that be a nice thing for them to do together? Viktor isn't sure if it would be a nice thing for him or for her, but he thanks her, steals a biro from a desk in the library and writes down each new recipe, from gratin aux aubergines to courgette-flower omelette.

And Jim, of course. Jim strolls through all the rooms as if the house belonged to him, helps himself to the German beer that Viktor and the *femme de ménage* have brought back from the autumn Oktoberfest market, and drinks it in the twilight of the pantry, where Viktor finds him as he goes in search of a jar of plums for the tajine. Lying on his back, he floats in the pool, naked, fanning the water gently with his white-haired limbs, and greets Viktor with the words: Aha, the young

German! Most often Viktor surprises him at Lionel's desk, bent over one of his drawings. Come here, my boy, he says, and pushes some of them towards Viktor. Blood-red and brown graffiti dissolve into chunks across the page, looking like a feeling that Viktor cannot quite remember. There's something in there, isn't there? Jim asks, it's not just nonsense. As Jim and Viktor discuss the picture, trying to decipher the carefully shaded letters, they are on the same side for a moment, and then Viktor says: *Putain.*

Jim raises his wobbly head and looks him in the face expectantly. *Putain?* he asks. That is there?

Time for me to throw you out now, Viktor starts, and grabs Jim's flaccid upper arm. You know full well that whatever's here does not concern you.

Haaa, the old man laughs and slips surprisingly easily out of Viktor's grasp. You should do your job, my boy.

At half-past six, Madame comes home and greets the children with a nervous cheerfulness that reminds Viktor of the hiking expedition in the Calanques. For Maud, who has taken to following Viktor all afternoon at every turn, grilling him about the life and death of crickets, snails or caterpillars, Viktor suddenly ceases to exit. For Lionel he has never existed anyway. The children show Madame their scrapes and school folders, and when Viktor goes into the kitchen to rinse the espresso maker and spin the salad ready for the starter, he hears the sound of her voice, slow and tired, from behind the closed door, talking about homework with one of the children.

His Matusja had never been concerned about his school stuff. But when she came home from the textile factory, she sometimes had embroidered pennants or a sports badge in her coat pocket, and in the carnival period, a large bag of fabric scraps which she would use to sew Arabian costumes late into the night. She barely sat with him in the children's room because she barely sat at all. But when he stood with her in the kitchen, helping her lay the table, she belonged entirely to him. He would let down the folding table and set out the dishes while she warmed up the sausages and cut bread. He would tell her about all the wonders and unbelievable things he experienced every day. That the old history teacher was now selling Lucky Strike in the kiosk on Karl-Marx-Allee, which is now called Kastanienallee, even though there are no chestnut trees there. Or that the new English teacher is actually the old Russian teacher, even though she speaks even worse English than Russian. He told her all that and other things, as long as it wasn't about his brother-in-law, and his Matusja laughed wearily, shook her head at the confused world out there and quietly rejoiced at the order in her own home. She would also shake her head over a lettuce spinner, Viktor thought, stirring the vinaigrette. Matusja's salads were wet and so sweet that the sugar crystals crunched between your teeth when you ate them.

Monsieur comes home later. Sometimes during the salad, sometimes only during the main course and sometimes when they are already on the cheese. He often arrives when Maud is already in bed. If she is still awake and hears the crunch of the motorbike tyres on the gravel of the courtyard, she jumps out of bed and scampers outside barefoot to fall into his arms. Lionel stays in his room. Monsieur isn't his father after all, the *femme de ménage* says once, as she rocks her tightly permed head between the books. They play their cards close to their chest in this family, don't they? Monsieur met Madame when Lionel was already two, she says, adroitly scooping up the bits of lint into her cloth. Viktor stands in the door frame, vacuum cleaner in hand. The suction noise seems to come from all walls at the same time, which must be due to the flue system. But he is still his father, in a way, Viktor insists, as if there might be a doubt there. And maybe it's because of the noise, but when the *femme de ménage* turns to him and yells: He loves him, *tu sais*! He loves him more than his own wife, her voice seems to break.

When Maud runs towards Monsieur in her nightdress, he lifts her up and twirls her round in a circle, so that her bare legs fly through the air. He nods politely and absent-mindedly to Viktor. Later, he disappears behind the narrow door to the room with the music system, turns on the speakers in the pool and puts on an album, Pink Floyd or Gong and occasionally an early Metallica, but no one hears it because, like Viktor, he mutes the speakers in the house. Then he strolls onto the night terrace and slides silently into the pool. And Viktor, who is still cleaning up in the kitchen, pauses briefly while rinsing the sink and looks at Monsieur's slow, regular strokes in the pool's coloured lights.

Viktor only stops watching Monsieur when he hears the whistle. Julija is standing in front of the garage, her white jeans hardly stand out from the courtyard gravel, her hair sticking out blurs with the darkness. Come with me, she says, her voice trembling, something's up with our *Did*.

The gap in the hedge seems to have widened since his arrival. Nevertheless, Viktor scratches his arms on the dry twigs. Jim lies on the other side, face down in the autumn lawn, his hands clamped to his ears.

When they turn him onto his back, they see he is conscious. A high-pitched whimper emanates from his tight-pressed lips, tears run down his unshaven cheeks. *Au secours!* screams Jim with a high voice, *zu Hilfe!* He takes turns screaming it in German and in French, and he is still screaming as Viktor carries him into the house and lays him down on his bed behind the kitchen. This blasted river, Jim groans when his head hits the pillow, shit, the water is cold!

Where is everyone? Viktor wants to know, as he presses Jim's huge hands into the mattress to calm him down, he cannot think of anything better to do. Benjamin is asleep, says Julija. His parents have gone for a drink. I'm drowning, Jim shouts, with tears running down his face, I'm drowning in this filthy sludge! Blast the capital! Blast all the French! I don't care!

He calms down only when Benjamin appears out of nowhere by his bed. He is barefoot and in a light-blue terry sleepsuit with a pattern of printed aeroplanes, his little face pale with terror, or does he always look like this, Viktor wonders as he lets go of the old man's hands. Benjamin climbs into Jim's bed and wraps his little arms around his fluttering chest. Hey, Grandpa, he says sleepily, I want to be a pilot, too. Benjamin says more, but that is lost in the old man's sobs, while the boy tucks himself under Jim's sweaty armpit and falls asleep as if nothing were out of the ordinary. When Julija finally finds the blanket in the bed box and throws it over them, Jim is only cursing softly. Tears and snot run down his chin, but he does not wipe them away because his grandson is sleeping under his armpit. As Viktor and Julija stand in the doorway, he mutters something to them, it sounds like: Otherwise it will burn . . . whatever happens protect . . . the rest is lost in the last of his sobs.

Julija and Viktor stand for a while on the doorstep looking at one another. The moon stands high above the pine trees in the front gardens, casting shadow on their faces that makes them look older than they are. Now would be the time to smoke a cigarette and say something profound. Get lost, says Julija and pushes Viktor towards the gate. Her voice still sounds shaky. And thank you, *Nazi boyfriend*.

Instead of taking the shortcut through the hedge, Viktor leaves via the courtyard gate.

☦

The night is a black snail. Maman is fast asleep. In her sleep, she presses my head to her chest. Her hands are heavy on my ears. I can still hear everything. In the next room, Lionel is crying. I also hear what I don't hear. No sound from Papa. He's next door too.

And I hear something else. Infinitely slowly, the courtyard gate open and closes. The crunch of footsteps in the yard. Someone is entering our house through the garage. Someone is coming up the stairs. Someone is trying to be quiet. Is it Jim? Someone stumbles on the stairs and curses in his language.

I unwind myself from Maman's vice-like grip. At the door I look round again. Her blonde hair spills over my pillow. She does not have small eyes in her sleep. Door handle down, out quietly, door closed.

In the hallway stands the au pair rubbing his ankle. I fly at him. I don't care if he thinks like a fighter. I slam both fists into his stomach. But it's like steel. He doesn't even flinch.

What's the matter? he asks.

But I can't say anything. Nothing at all. And in the silence of my saying nothing, he finally hears Lionel.

The au pair rips open Lionel's door. Papa is lying on his back. He has his eyes closed and his arms crossed behind his head. His penis stands huge and erect. Lionel is crouching in front of his penis. His bare shoulders jerking weirdly. For a moment, Papa and Lionel look like Jim's medal on the wall. Or like an animal with six legs. But it's worse than that. They look like Papa and Lionel.

And then several things happen at once. Lionel gets up and jumps off the bed. The spider disintegrates. Papa throws himself to one side and covers his penis. The au pair stands over him and starts hitting him.

That's all that happens after that. The au pair rains blows down onto Papa who is curled up like a snail. Papa raises his arms over his head and starts crying like Lionel. The fist still keeps smashing into his face, his hairy belly, his side. The au pair overwhelms him. And me? I'm everywhere and nowhere. I push myself between the au pair and Papa. He mustn't kill Papa. I hear loud sobs. Is that me?

Lionel has closed his eyes. He squats under the window and leans his head against the wall. He's waiting. But I don't know what for.

Suddenly it stops. Maman is standing in the doorway. Blinking. Now she looks like Gerda. Her and no one else. With her hand outstretched, she walks towards Papa and the au pair. She pulls Papa off the bed and says, Come on.

She is holding him up him like he's a grandpa, though Papa is certainly only half Jim's age. But you can't see that right now because his face is swollen. They stagger out of Lionel's room.

14

Had Madame not intervened, he would still be at it: beating Monsieur to a pulp. He would be smashing his bloody fist into his skull, time and again, until his sick brain seeped out in a defenceless mush. Pull yourself together, says Viktor into the darkness of the stairwell, just give this shit a rest. But his thoughts well out of him, as if he had hammered a hole in his own head. There's no Marcel here to pull him off and whisk him away in a fast car. No chance of getting away with it again, Viktor thinks. Here, you're not in the East.

Viktor unclenches his fists from his forehead and looks around in the darkness. The doors to the children's rooms are only ajar, their bedside lamps cut narrow lines of light into the stairwell. He hadn't been able to take them in his arms—or whatever it is you do when one of them has just seen the other being fucked in the mouth by their father. He sits on the stairs and feels something moist across the knuckles of his right hand. It tastes like blood, and Viktor doesn't know whether it is his or Monsieur's.

The door to Ruth's grandfather's room had also been open. For the first time since he's been here, Viktor thinks of Ruth. But not Ruth in the strobe light of the shoe factory, whose swaying body appeared somewhere different with every flash of light, not her cool gaze and not the way she disappeared so casually, when he so badly needed her to get him out of there, not he get her out. Viktor thinks of Ruth in the middle of the snowy winter of her childhood. Come over to ours, she had said, chewing the clumps of ice off her mittens, from Grandpa's attic you can see your block! He can still hear the creaking of his winter boots on the old wooden steps of the stairwell, see his small hand, red with cold, sliding up the bannister.

Behind the white-painted door of the apartment, he recognized Ruth's light steps. Happy that she was there, he pressed the bell. Nothing stirred. He rang again. Her mother was probably at work, but why didn't Ruth open the door? Viktor got down on his knees and lifted the iron flap of the letter box to peer into the apartment. Too dark to recognize anything. On the spur of the moment he pressed the handle down.

The hallway light was off, Ruth's winter anorak hung between large coats in the semi-darkness of the coat pegs, onto which a narrow strip of light fell from the living room. Victor heard hushed sounds that had his heart in his throat. A low moaning and sighing, a rustling in a rhythm that Viktor knew but also did not. He took a step closer and looked through the gap of the door. Ruth's grandfather sat in the armchair next to the radio. She stood in front of him holding up her dress as if she were catching stars. Viktor turned round and ran out of the apartment.

Did she know he was there? She must have heard the ringing. The door shutting and falling into the catch behind him. Had she really not been aware of anything? Not even as he tumbled down the stairs in panic? If so, she knew he had run away.

Chort! Espèce de yellow arsehole, Viktor curses into the darkness. He suddenly realizes how scary it must be for the children that the guy who has just beaten up their father is now sitting in the stairwell and, *lâche!*, talking to himself. But this time he hasn't run away. He is still there, guarding the two children as they sleep—each of whom almost certainly hate him, though each for a different reason.

Of course, they are not asleep. They lie curled up in their beds, each in their own room, carefully checking whether their bodies are still there. Hands, arms, shoulders. Legs, thighs, chest. The au pair's curses in the stairwell flutter like moths against the light, or simply like little shreds of nothing.

‡

Lionel and I put ourselves to bed. He's in his, I'm in mine. The wall separating us.

We listen to the sounds. That's the front door. That's the key. This is Maman's car. That's the gate. That's the way to the hospital.

The au pair sits outside our rooms in the hallway. He is taking care of us. That's what he is learning our language for. It has nothing to do with his girlfriend. Except that he came from her, I think.

Now I know. The answer to Jim's question, whether the au pair also thinks like a fighter. He doesn't. He thinks like a child. In fact, that's the best thing about him.

I can see him through the open door. He is curled up on the stairs, in the semi-darkness, his head in his hands. He's there, and he's not there. The night is hollow inside.

15

The truly extreme events are lost to memory. The brain places a fog over the earth's surface of your memory, which would reveal some things, if it really mattered to you. But it doesn't. You race across the continents on a train that departed long ago, trying hard to see nothing, nothing at all, in the fog. A free ticket from the brain that everyone who is offered it takes without a thought.

Either that or you remember them with absolute clarity. Viktor will remember France as if he were looking through binoculars, just held the wrong way around. The numbers in the lift of the Clara Schumann Hospital are absolutely clear as he goes up the five floors to Surgery II. The lights along the corridor by the nurses' station are absolutely clear but far, far away, and as if it were not all of him in the hallway but only his eyes. The green walls on the right and left pass him by in absolute clarity; in front of the nurse's room stands the trolley, with small metallic instruments on it, which flash and disappear in the darkness of the house, in which a part of him is still sitting on the stairs talking to himself. *Vse po poryadku*, Viktor says to himself, because it calms him. As if from a great distance, but somehow with absolute clarity, he opens the door to Room 105 for what Madame called a conversation to clear things up with the man he beat to a pulp only twelve hours ago.

It is a well-lit room that does not fit the faces of those present. The cloudless October sky falls through the window onto yellow-painted walls and shiny linoleum. A drip stands next to Monsieur's bed with a bag of clear liquid dangling from it. On the table in a bowl with a pattern of cicadas, which Viktor recognizes, are vitamin bars, fruit and crackers. Madame sits on a chair by the edge of the bed and looks terrified, as if she has not specially asked Viktor to come. The head of the bed is raised, the pillow freshly plumped. On it lies Monsieur, lost in thought, looking out of the window strenuously. With a broken jaw, contusion on his left cheekbone, a black eye and ruptured gallbladder, it is probably not altogether easy to look out of the window like that, Viktor thinks, and clears his throat. *Bonjour*, he says, and stops himself from adding *ça va*. Should I get the police? asks the nursing assistant, appearing from nowhere. She is standing at the sink behind the built-in cupboard, disinfecting her hands. That's him, she says, am I right? Yes, no, says Madame and raises her trembling hands, that's him, but we don't want . . . Don't put up with aggression like that! cries the assistant in a shrill voice, and her coiffure starts quivering. With a contemptuous flash of her eyes in Viktor's direction, she storms past him and slams the door shut behind her.

They are alone. Monsieur is still looking out of the window. Madame blinks nervously. We need to talk, she says.

Yes, says Viktor.

And Madame starts to explain that she has experienced all sorts of things, especially in a profession like hers. Traumatized victims who become perpetrators. Perpetrators, she says, evading Viktor's gaze, who behave just like children. Deep developmental disorders in the midst of healthy families. This goes through all strata of society, Victoire, she says, and glances distractedly at Monsieur, who is still looking out of the window. Viktor is not sure if Monsieur hears what is being said; maybe he has smashed his ear canal or something. But then he sees his tight-pressed lips twitching above the bandage on his chin. But, Madame says, that they should end up taking in someone like that, a case like that, and, what is more, into the bosom of their family, she looks at her hands resting in in her lap, she would never have thought. Not in her wildest dreams. She takes a sip from the coffee cup standing behind her on the windowsill and folds her hands again. Her finger joints protrude white. She and her husband had shown forbearance when they took him in, even though he had come by the job as au pair with, *comment dire*, a ridiculous lie. As if they wouldn't have taken a young man! Where do we live, Madame asks, stiffening her back, if not in an enlightened Europe! Encouraged by her own speech, she looks Viktor in the eye briefly; Monsieur too nods imperceptibly. Not even the fact that he looked like a real *salaud de Nazi* had stopped them. They didn't care how people at school talked about the East German giant, who popped out of the bushes barefoot every afternoon to take her children home. If her daughter had not developed a soft spot for him, this traumatized hobgoblin, he would not have stayed a month. A chance, says Madame, and looks past Viktor, they have given him a chance. But he took the first opportunity—to do what? And with a glance at her husband, as if to reassure herself that it really is so, Madame continues: You beat him up. Out of the blue. For no reason. In front of the children.

Everything spins in Viktor's head and drives away the fog. Facts swirl. His fist, bearing down on Monsieur, who is imploring him with his eyes to stop. Lionel with his legs wrapped round him in the corner of the room. His jerky movements on Monsieur's erect penis. Madame! he says with a voice that is too high to sound controlled. Your son . . . Monsieur was fu . . . .

Don't you dare, says Madame. I don't want to hear what lies you're concocting in your pathological state. No one will file a complaint. You won't, and we won't. For my husband and me, the children come first. We want you, Madame says with a voice that breaks on the freshly cleaned panorama window, we want you to leave our house immediately.

Viktor's body is too small for this space. His arms are too long, his voice too loud for Surgery II. With a moan which scares even him, because it reminds him of the moaning of his brother-in-law, he reaches into the hospital bed. Why don't you say anything, you arsehole? he shouts in three languages and grabs Monsieur by the throat. Why don't you say anything, you paedo bastard? At that moment two carers drag him off and bring him to his knees with practised blows to the kidneys. Nice and quiet, gently does it, he hears from behind him. Be glad that your victim is refusing to press charges. And now piss off.

The last thing Viktor sees as the carers drag him out of Room 105 is Monsieur who, submerged in shame and relief, curls into his sheets, staring at the signet ring on his right hand.

And the first thing he hears after he is dumped in front of the automatic entrance door of the hospital: Here he is, the strapping German!

Jim is standing directly under the 'No Smoking' sign and laughing toothlessly at Viktor. In one hand he holds his drip, on which hangs, in addition to the obligatory clear liquid (blood thinner, Jim explains), a urine bag, the contents of which glow like amber in the autumn sun. Cardio 1, Jim explains, clogged aorta. With the cigarillo in the other hand he points at his chest, as if he were shooting himself in the heart, and adds: You understand? Viktor nods. The sky above the Clara Schumann Hospital draws together and clears again, shreds of clouds race at high speed over the figures in front of the entrance, which opens with each visitor and closes again like a heart valve, or just like only months earlier the door at the railway station had opened and closed behind Viktor's back.

Jim hands Viktor a cigarillo. When he lights it for him, his great hand trembles. They stand next to each other in silence and draw the biting smoke into their lungs. Why are you visiting me anyway? Jim asks, and straightens up a little on his drip stand to give Viktor a searching stare. And before Viktor can clear up the misunderstanding, he adds: Boy, promise me one thing. Take care of the children. Oh, and while you're at it, you might as well give that *crétin de père* something to write home about.

He has already done that, the bloody idiot, says Julija. As if conjured out of thin air, she stands in front of Jim and Viktor, hair sticking out in all directions round her pale face. Lionel and Maud stand next to her, trying hard to look normal. *Mon cher Didu*, says Julija, and bends down to kiss Jim's cheeks. If you knew what went on last night, your own life would seem uneventful by comparison. And to Viktor: Idiot! If they throw you out now, Lionel has no one to get him out of the shit.

That's what they've just done, says Viktor, and that moment gets a resounding slap from Julija.

A high tone rings in his head and mixes with the howl of a siren that pulls in just in front of A&E next to them, while Maud tugs on his arm and asks: Victoire? Victoire!

When Viktor can hear again, Julija is setting Jim straight on the current state of affairs: . . . Just on our way from the Youth Office. They are pressing charges. Don't worry, Jim. I'll take care of . . .

Victoire? says Maud, looking up at Viktor. How big she looks, the thought shoots through his mind. Can you grow up in a single night? He embraces her small body and lifts her up. Maud snuggles her head against his neck, as feather-light as ever. She smells of salt and gummy bears. You're not going to go away, are you? she says. *Si tu restes, je te donne ma collection des coquilles.*

Above them, the shreds of clouds race, as if the world has started spinning faster since the night before. Viktor holds Maud in his arms and turns to Lionel, who stands behind them in a blind spot. The boy clings to the padded straps of his backpack and looks from Julija to Jim, and from Jim, for once, to Viktor. His face is white, as if he were the heart patient and not Jim, and that is true, in a way. Because, yes, you can grow up overnight. Or as if he were the moon, standing motionless in the darkness. A satellite moon spinning in the light and shadow of the larger body, completely unable to move under its own volition. Exactly, Viktor thinks, without being able to put it into words in any language. That's the feeling that the writing on his desk reminded him of, *putain*.

And what are we going to do about this? Madame asks, blinking.

The tiredness sits in her eyes like a grain of Saharan sand blown by the mistral to Europe to cause minor insurance damage to car bodies or just to cause infinite fatigue. Her question is directed at the head of the au pair agency, who is just as tired and sits in the check-in area of the Marseilles Provence Airport, waiting for her flight to Palermo to see her youngest daughter's newborn. Children, she says on the phone, are our primary concern. Of course, we must protect them.

Naturellement, Madame reiterates slowly, and of course it is out of the question to set a violent perpetrator loose on them. Have you reported it? If I did, Madame says, I assure you it would be the end of your agency.

We will deal with this discreetly, mutters the lady from the au pair agency, whose name has just been read out for Last Calls.

I'll tell you what we're going to do now, Madame says, stifling a yawn. The Saharan grain of fatigue is making her eyelids heavy. She saw Monsieur's open flies, she is not blind. But the reality in this case is only one version of events, and it doesn't make things worse than they have been for a long time. Close your eyes and get through this, Madame thinks to herself and says: My mother-in-law is collecting the children from school today. When the three of them come home, the boy will be gone. I am relying on you. Goodbye.

Through the terminal window, the au pair placement officer watches the plane to Palermo, which has just left its position on the stand. She was so looking forward to taking a nap on the plane. Something is wrong with this family, but she can't quite put her finger on it. Besides which, she is tired, endlessly tired. In the sky above the runway, clouds chase each other in confusing formations. Hard to say who the hunter is and who the hunted.

Viktor will remember France the way one remembers something after which nothing is as it was before. With absolute clarity he sees himself fetch the backpack with the crane emblem from his room. A few letters from home, a handful of photos, including the one of Lionel in the Calanques twirling Maud around. He looks straight out of the picture and seems to shout to him, and only to him: Don't go away! But Viktor knows, of course, that Lionel was actually shouting something else. Maïe's notebook for recipes, a hunk of baguette from the morning, an Italian salami and a litre of milk. He stuffs everything into a plastic bag fetched from the pantry behind the kitchen.

With absolute clarity, Viktor sees himself go through the house from top to bottom. The children's beds lie rumpled in the semi-darkness of their rooms, the wooden shutters closed. Viktor pulls their doors to with care, as if they were here and could still stop him. On the telephone table in the library, he discovers one of Monsieur's credit cards. He tucks it into his jacket. On the stone floor of the laundry cellar lie white globules. Some of the drawers of the homeopathic home pharmacy cabinet are open because Madame gave the children placebos after her return from the emergency room.

As always, the door to the garage is unlocked. Monsieur's MV Agusta gives off a reddish sheen in the faint light that falls through the slits of the lowered garage door.

With absolute clarity, Viktor sees the white gravel spurting up to the side as he roars out of the yard. The gate closes behind him as he accelerates, ignoring the bollards. In the bend, the plastic bag slips off the handlebars, and the salami, the baguette, and Matusja's letters with their fine slanting Cyrillic handwriting fly onto the tarmac. But Viktor doesn't stop.

Later, when the lady from the au pair agency parks in front of the house to make sure that the problem case has cleared out of her clients' house, she finds nothing but an unreadable wad of paper in the gutter in front of the house. And the violent au pair is long gone.

Viktor sees himself heading north, on the Autoroute du Sud. He has only ridden a motorbike once in his life, between the rustling cornfields of home, on a bike belonging to a friend of Marcel's, but has remembered the basics. When he finally looks up, the ridge of the Montagne Sainte-Victoire has disappeared behind him. Should he keep going north? East? It doesn't really matter, he thinks, and chooses a road at random. The villages become smaller and greyer, the solar body make a final effort to warm the harvested fields around him. As if from high above, Viktor sees himself driving along the dead straight road, a red dot on the map of the Bouches-du-Rhône, moving as if it were aiming towards a goal.

When Viktor sees the flames on the horizon, he thinks: that doesn't matter either. A few fields are alight, and he has no idea whether the farmers are burning them in the fall to renew the soil, or whether the apocalypse is imminent. Viktor just heads for the blaze. As the flames are licking at the edges of the road to left and right of him, it dawns on him that there is no one to whom he can tell this story. The police won't believe someone like him. Nor the au pair agency, which has no doubt already received a call from Madame. Not his parents, who have told all the neighbours in the block about their successful son abroad. Not even Marcel, who has no idea anyway. And not Julija, whom he will not see again. Julija with the crazy laugh. Julija with the slap. He wouldn't have to tell her anything, she would just know . . . And there's no one he can tell about the overwhelming helplessness he feels for having left Maud and Lionel behind. (If you stay, I'll give you my snail collection.) And no one to tell that the night before, for once in his life, he did the right thing.

If anyone, Ruth.

III

Voitto

1

Time for you to appear, Voitto. This initial applause does not last long, and this is your last chance to make it to your seat, if you are standing at the hall door and not coming in. Of course, you will come in. All the doorkeepers here know that you belong with me. This city of half a million inhabitants is smaller than you would like. Everyone knows everyone. You, Ruth, you would say. Everyone knows you.

If it isn't working, Mother had said, just lie on your back. Lie on your back and take a deep breath. Or in your words: fat floats. But that was in the middle of the never-ending winter-summer of my childhood, when Fly was still there shooting at the legs of the neighbour's chickens with his air rifle; when I was still playing a quarter-size violin and thought a slap was the natural conclusion to an argument; when time, laughter, crying and having to stand still had no beginning and no end. So, long before I met you. I don't think of you now, or not only of you. I think of my mother in her dark-blue swimsuit. Or was it purple? Or green and blue stripes? It may be that I picture some of this differently from how it was, my memory is colour blind. But Voitto, I am not lying when I tell you, even if it is only today and here, in front of the dark orchestra pit, in the darkness of my thoughts, how it felt then.

There was a lightness about lying on your back staring up into the late-afternoon sky circling above. Fly and I paddled the water with our hands so as not to sink and drifted as quietly as possible on the surface of the dredging lake. That's brilliant, Mother said, and stroked her hand over my flat chest. Deep breaths, Ruth, then you can't sink. Yes, that's it!

There was a lightness about being dead among the mid-summer clouds. Ears just below the surface of the water, I heard the vibrations as Fly and Mother moved around, floating beside me, maybe I also heard the slow waving of the fins of the carp in the deeper layers and, at the bottom, the gravel slippages, which the sign on the shore warned about. Attention, open water, parents are liable for their children. Last summer, said Fly, a child drowned here. Swam out alone, and halfway out to the island, the sand deep below him started to move. Ruth? asked Fly with his especially friendly voice, do you know what happens when there is a slippage deep below us? I didn't know, and Fly said: It creates a whirlpool. A small but powerful whirlpool. It sucks you down into the depths before you can even scream.

It is possible to put that in a less scary way, my dear, Mother interjected and sprayed Fly in the face with a handful of water. True! he spluttered and wiped the spit from his chin.

Later when I lifted my head to make sure that Fly and Mother were still there, because it had become so quiet around me, my legs sank down into the colder layers of the lake, and I saw our mother lying on her back, her blonde hair splayed out on the surface, the polyester mountains of her breasts mimicking the midsummer clouds high above us and her arms spread out as if she were embracing not just the sky but the sense of lightness itself.

You do not find me fat. At most a bit serious. And not exactly with a gift for the gab. It is just a saying, you say. How can you joke with someone who sees every comment as a criticism? You may not speak much, Ruth, but your body speaks for you. You clearly have inherited your breasts from your mother. But where, you ask me, do you get your silence from?

A question for you in return, Voitto. Where are you? I am up here; I'm enduring the welcome applause and I'm really quite easy to find. It was a joke, Voitto, especially for you. I recognize my old music teacher, who winks enthusiastically at me, and I pretend not to have noticed her. Pap and Mother have seats in the front row and are looking down at their hands in their laps. Mother, because she is embarrassed to be the centre of attention, but I know that she is looking forward to hearing me in a minute. The seat next to her is empty. Pap, because he is in inner dialogue with God—with God and his concern for Fly—a concern which, given half a chance, will drive him out of the room before I have even started. I think briefly of my brother too, until I realize that the empty seat is not reserved for him after all, because I knew that he would not come. It is for you.

Gravity can be handled one way or another. It is the force of a mass that is always greater than you. It is the power of the heavier body over the lighter one. It is the most reliable force I know. It simply never stops. A year after Mother and I had moved back in with Pap and Fly, Grandfather was suddenly standing at the door. It was a mild winter's day, the frost flowers on the staircase window had not yet covered the glass. Not exactly cardigan weather. Grandfather's dry body shivered with cold as he scurried into the apartment, with his slippers leaving a smudge of damp leaves. Mother jumped when she saw him. Mummy, he called to her, as if he had just been at the front and was coming home. The war is over!

He is the second man in my family who moved in with his daughter wearing only a cardigan over his shirt. Perhaps that is what you do if you can see no other way. The end of reason arrives inappropriately dressed and moves in with its own children. Not the worst thing you can do.

It took a while before Grandfather would finally lie down. Until then, he kept scurrying back and forth through our apartment as if through the decades of his life, striving for an impeccable attitude. During the day, the snot ran down over his mouth and chin until my mother hurried up to him and held one of his large cloth handkerchiefs under his nose, into which he snorted unpleasantly, as if he couldn't care less. At night I heard him groaning like an old child. Hermann, he sobbed and buried his wet face in his huge hands. Hermann, I can't find the blasted capsule!

Once he suddenly turned up behind me in the attic, I was in the middle of the opening of the third movement, presto agitato, of Beethoven's *Moonlight* Sonata, which I had found in the school library. I was playing the right-hand part and humming the left-hand bass line as Grandfather laid his cool hand on my neck. Bow in the air, I span around.

Here you are, he said, and started fiddling uncertainly with his flies. Don't you love your daddy any more?

After Grandfather had finally given himself over to the dead, my mother took two codeine at once, lay down in bed and slept two days straight. When she woke up, Pap was at her bedside with a plate full of flour soup in his hand. The soup was cold because it had taken him quite a while to wake Mother up; the milk had formed a skin over the surface with sugar crystals. Fly and I stood behind the half-open door, trying hard not to intrude.

What are you doing here? Mother asked sleepily and coughed.

Pap shrugged his shoulders. Just checking to see if God is listening, he muttered. When you actually ask him for something.

Never ask, stupid, Mother murmured. At most say thank you.

And Pap said, Okay.

2

Gravity can be handled one way or another, Fly said the last time I saw him. He was standing at the stage entrance of the Gewandhaus and already had his backpack on, with his sleeping mat and camera bag strapped to the sides, which gave him the outline of an action hero against the light in the hallway. An action hero with a full beard, because when his hair started falling out, he shaved the rest and grew a beard to compensate, which made him look like a mixture of a GDR clergyman and a rapper. Like someone who knows how to express himself when he wants to be taken seriously.

Either you accept things the way they are, he said, putting the hip belt on, or you climb against them. He had his upright posture from our grandfather, it occurred to me. Despite the weight on his back, he stood ramrod straight and was laughing at me. From whom did he have his lightness? In the background, two men were rolling the Bechstein onto the stage, in three hours I had my concert, in ten minutes the stage rehearsal would begin.

Aren't you afraid of falling or something? I asked.

From the treehouse? Fly laughed. I'm more afraid that the camera will be confiscated.

The treehouses that Fly was joining were built in the canopy of an oak forest a few kilometres from our old house. It is not the 'Russian Forest' of our childhood, though, whose horizon glowed red beyond the tank entrance at the edge of the village, when the Soviets had set the heath on fire during their war games. All the unexploded bombs on the forest floor that accumulated over the years, the hand grenades in the overgrown bunkers, all the lost ammunition in the mycelium of the red caps and puffballs, all the unexploded chemical dumps, even the forgotten caches of rocket warheads or the mere rumour of them—all these now belong to a nature reserve, which is no longer officially called 'Russian Forest'. Such a wilderness cannot easily be cleared without risking explosions. At best you can create cycling maps, following the paths of the wolves that have returned to the area but are rarely seen. Only in spring do you see them sometimes standing on the edge of the airfield howling at the afternoon moon, Fly claimed once.

Is there really an airfield in the Russian Forest? I wanted to know.

Sure, Fly said, a hundred acres. If you had ever put your violin away, I would have shown you the underground command centre.

Show it to me now.

Man, you really do come home too seldom. It's long gone.

Fly was going to be winched up to treehouses in one of the neighbouring forests. In the endless summers of our childhood, Pap had sometimes organized community trips there. One left the village behind the agricultural cooperative sheds, past the former mill and straight along beside the ditch, Fly and I racing ahead of everyone else, frightening the grey herons with our noise, because we knew the way by heart. Onwards between the fields, then into the forest, like entering a cool green bowl, where we immediately disappeared among the trunks of the oaks, hooting and shouting, while the adults got out thermos flasks and traybakes.

Hold your horses, Voitto. No one is saying that everything used to be better then. Fly is my witness that a lot has changed. If you want to go to the forest today, you must show your ID, empty your bags and, if you look like my brother, strip down to your underpants. The local district has a contract with the Central German Lignite Company to clear the forest. But the treehouses, connected by ropes and improvised bridges suspended at a height of ten metres, have put a halt to the process. There are composting toilets, small gas cookers, and tinned vegetables from the nearby supermarkets, but no ladders down from the trees. If you want to leave your treehouse, you must abseil down securely.

But I don't come down any more, Fly said. The cops have taken to standing under my tree kicking their heels. But after the end of their shift, Dummy-doll, once they are gone, the bats swoop between our huts, and then we can finally take our masks off and get drunk on nothing but fresh air. Come and visit us, he added. If they close the forest, we will put you in touch with the people in the Aktion Unterholz group.

What do they do? I wanted to know.

None of the big stuff, Fly said, looking at his watch. Breeching police cordons and stuff like that.

Fly?

Yes.

My brother had already turned to go. On his backpack was a badge with the crane logo of the East Elbe District Transport Company, which was supporting the protests. It reminded me of something but I couldn't put my finger on it.

Where do you get the courage from? I wanted to know.

Are you joking? He retorted. I'm afraid of heights!

I couldn't believe my ears.

Didn't you know? he asked, glancing at his watch again. But first, you always have to climb against it. Anything that drags you down. Do you understand, Dummy-doll? And second, they demolished our village.

Where our house once stood, there is now an East Elbe Grand Canyon. Where once I used to hide in our attic to play violin, there are expanses of cloudless sky. In place of the community room, a shovel-wheel excavator digs the coal seams out of vast craters. Swifts dart through the place where Pap made his campfire under the apple trees; instead of the tops of the apple trees, the air stands in the midday heat.

The day the church was taken away was a Thursday in October. With an unlit pipe in his mouth, Pap stood behind a British structural engineer whose instructions he would not have understood even if he had been able to speak English. Instead, he kept his gaze fixed on the twelve hydraulic presses that were used to lift the building so that the transport company could manoeuvre its forty axles underneath. Next to him, beer in hand, stood our neighbour. Pap slowly turned his face. And just as the neighbour was about to pat him on the shoulder with a collegial gesture, Pap said: It was about time.

The neighbour looked at him and didn't understand immediately.

That your blasted waterpipes, Pap said calmly, were levelled to the ground.

The cordons fluttered in front of the heaps of rubble; Mother stood behind a folding table, handing out hot cocoa as if it were the St Martin's Day celebrations. In extreme situations we draw on routine, and making cocoa runs in the family. The sign marking the end of the village had been removed at the last minute. When the church passed the place it had stood, to loud applause from the onlookers, the journalists put their cameras on pause and slammed their car doors to follow the convoy. Only Fly stood on the rubble of the former diocese office and kept his eyes fixed on the church tower, which became smaller and smaller between the fields and dismantled high-voltage power lines. After the convoy had disappeared over the horizon, he panned to his mother, who had put down her thermos and was wiping a tear from her cheek.

A year later, his film was shown at the Venice Biennale. In a camera pan, Viktor comes into shot out of nowhere. He has pulled up the zip of his parka and put his hands in his jeans pockets. Of course, he no longer wears a bomber jacket. When the camera is directly above him, he raises his hand like a concertgoer, and for a short time it looks as if he is about to give a Hitler salute. But then he stretches two fingers out of his clenched fist and forms them into the peace sign sign as a greeting to Fly, who probably did not even notice him amid everything that was going on. Then the camera is already on the move again; Viktor is out of the picture.

Hundreds of people wept along during the scene with Mother, and in the subsequent Q&A, the selling-off of land in the service of an outmoded means of energy production was loudly denounced. But Mother, who sat proudly in the audience, spoke out, deliberately ignoring Fly's quiet shame. What a magnificent technical effort—all to preserve our beautiful church, she exclaimed with joy. It made me weep!

Such a magnificent technical effort, the simultaneous translator in his booth intoned (misunderstanding), it made you want to weep.

After Fly said his goodbyes, he took the S-Bahn in the direction of Eichenwald. Along with hundreds of other protesters, he got off at the final stop, which still bears the name of our village, although hardly any of the younger ones arriving from all over the country knows that this village ever existed. The stories are coming to an end and cannot hold up the march of time. Why stand against it?

not even you believe yourself that indifference of yours (rolling-eye emoji), Fly wrote to me from the queue by the checks, (baby emoji) there are good reasons to fight back.

I discussed the stage plan for that evening's concert with the director of the Gewandhaus. The concert hall was sold out, but as always when I played at home, I had reserved a place for Mother and Pap in the front row so they could watch the concert without being distracted by thinking about Fly. It was not until after the final applause, when they stood around in my dressing room for a while and watched me pack my things, that I switched off flight mode on the phone.

i'm inside now, Fly wrote. already seen a bechstein's bat (rolling on the floor laughing emoji).

ha ha, I wrote back. call that a joke? And put on my jacket.

what's with the joke-police, hey? Fly wrote back. loads of cops about here too.

it's better here than it used to be, Fly wrote me a week later. I was sitting in the wings of a studio stage in Hilversum, going through the *presto* again and waiting for the violins to come back from their lunchbreak, when my phone started vibrating.

Fly: there are blueberries and wild juniper.

Me: never picked blueberries.

Fly: of course you haven't.

Me: and if you need anything else? like drinking water?

Fly: the supporters on the ground bring it. they even charge our portable generator.

Me: (thumbs-up emoji)

Fly: (baby emoji) could be you don't hear from me for a while. tomorrow is a big deployment. they want to use machines and cut us out of the trees.

Me: ???

Fly: don't worry (bee emoji) happy. we will shift one level higher right up into the canopy, it really sways up there.

Me: and then?

Fly: then log-in.

Me: what's that??

Fly: chain ourselves right up. takes up to 24h to unlock them.

Me: can i call in a mo?

Fly: tell them not to worry.

Me: hold on, i'll ring

Fly: dummy-doll

Me: give me 2 mins: i'll be done here, then i'll call

Fly: my fear of heights is gone. (laugh until you cry emoji)

As the conductor entered the studio stage and held up his hand for a high-five, Fly could not be reached.

In flight mode, you cannot be intercepted or tracked. But I'm not worried. Fly is the oldest activist on the ground and a local, he knows the oak forest like the back of his hand. I imagine him sitting in the canopy of the imperial oak, where we used to have our diocese picnic, keeping the police presence on the forest floor at bay through the dense foliage. Your brother doesn't really do things by halves, Pap said on the phone before the concert, and I told him what Fly had told me: Don't worry.

That is all I know. Fly's story is not over just because I don't know the end. Because Fly cannot be dictated to. From his canopy, through the fabric of his mask, he will be making his conditions known. It may not be easy to understand. But someone like Fly knows how to express himself in the face of destiny in a way that is unmistakably clear.

3

I have already spent far too long standing at the edge of the stage looking out for you. The right-hand door at the back of the stalls opens again, but instead of you I see a couple come in, feeling their way forward, apologetically, to their places.

Once we arrived late for your uncle's birthday party; he was a Finnish meat merchant, who made his lemon ice cream with vodka and basically assumed that everyone else would be having a good time too. When we finally arrived, the family was already eating their dessert. I was wearing sunglasses because of my swollen eyes; and a scarf round my neck to cover the bruises. I looked like a victim from *Vampire Diaries*. And because it is easier to lie when you include a grain of truth, you said to your uncle: The hotel bed collapsed. Ruth and I have been trying to put it together all this time.

Haw haw! your uncle guffawed and turned to your relatives. This young couple's bed collapsed! Very impressive!

The fact that the slatted base beneath the mattress did not break because we had been shagging so vigorously is the part you kept to yourself. We kept the truth between the two of us.

Have I ever told you that I find you most beautiful when you are angry? Your face above me framed by dark curls is even paler than usual. You press your lips together, moan and throw me onto my back. And in this brief moment of being overpowered, you are as close to me as the composer to his composition, or the person eating to the animal whose flesh he eats—or a pair of lovers for whom things are deadly serious.

You really mean that seriously, Ruth, you said once. I was sitting on the window seat in my room at the ITC Grand Central looking out at the low sky above Mumbai so as to avoid seeing my own camera image as you grilled me. Sheets of rain were beating down onto the equipment in a flooded playground between the Ashok Towers. A small red slide led directly into the water, as if this were an outdoor swimming pool and not a residential complex. Yes, everything is fine for you, you said, and your three-day beard twisted into a scornful grin. Sitting nice and comfy in your air-conditioned room looking out at the monsoon, while people a few kilometres away don't even have running water. But you weren't really talking about the water.

I tried to defend myself, it's different with B. than with you. No, not better. Just different. B. has always sung differently from you. More precise in timekeeping and then all those expansive gestures, that's why people take to him, I justify my stage partner as if he needed defending and not me. But Voitto, you have a different repertoire anyway! What does your music have to do with a Schubert song recital, apart from the fact that I play the piano part?

Your camera image froze and showed you pixelated and pale, staring past me with the dark moon shadows of your beard. The crackling of your microphone revealed that the connection was still working. Of course, it's great to be doing an Asian tour with B., I admitted. But B. is not you, Voitto.

Who comes to your concerts, anyway?

It depends, I responded evasively. Today mainly cultural people. The head of the Goethe-Institut, people in the diplomatic service, a few Indian poets in wide cotton shirts. They always get up in the middle of the concert to stretch their legs.

You laugh. I have known you for so long that I can also hear what you don't say. And before that? you want to know. Where were you again?

Kozhikode, Kerala, I said. For the opening concert. It was free of charge, and because there was no barrier to the beach promenade, more and more people kept swarming over—at least after 'The Trout'. In the end it was about three thousand, I guess. But probably they were there because of Amitabh Bachchan, who was on after us.

Anita who? you asked with the robotic sound of broken frequencies in your voice. The connection was getting worse. Your face had disappeared, and through the dark screen I caught sight of myself trying to look beautiful for you—just in case you could still see me.

Oh, I said, smiling at you, just some Bollywood actor.

In front of my window, the upper floors of the Ashok Towers were stuck fast in the monsoon clouds, or was it smog, or was it your silence, Voitto? Everything gets confused when

I think of you, I'm telling this whole story to you and no one else. The rain was lashing down on the playground equipment belonging to the condominium. An Indian couple ran towards one of the towers. They were holding plastic bags over their heads with one hand, and with the other holding the hand of a child between them, four years old perhaps; laughing, they were swinging the child high over the biggest puddles so that her short legs flew through the air. Suddenly Viktor came to mind—Viktor as he was when I met him. His wrinkled laughter that frightened all other four-year-olds. Just not me. Funnily enough, Viktor was the only constant in my life that I was never afraid of, even when I had reason to be. The funny thing is that I was afraid of all the other people and things even when there was no reason.

Voitto? Are you there?

The sound of the rain outside mixed with the noise of the air conditioning in my room and the hum of the laptop cooling on my sweaty knees. When did I stop feeling anything? Suddenly, like a short, frighteningly high-pitched tone, the answer came out of the fog of my memory and lay on the tip of my tongue.

Once I said: It's great that you have chosen to become a teacher. Young people need someone like you!

It sounded nice. But I know exactly what winds you up. You were always pretty serious, Voitto. B., the baritone I was accompanying on his Asian tour, was a tall, smooth-shaven guy with white sneakers whom you and I knew from the masterclass in London. At first we used to laugh together about the, as we saw it, gormlessness with which B. set about acquiring the romantic repertoire. For you, he was the living cliché of someone who would sooner or later sell his soul to a neoclassical label, a David Garrett of singing, who would never emerge from the shadow of the series of greats with whom he had studied. We, that much was clear, were in a different league. In high school, we worked late into the night on a version of Orff's 'The Moon' for two pianos and percussion, chorus, tenor and baritone. From my seat in the wings, I looked at your pale face, immersed in your score with absolute concentration, as if all this were a matter of life and death, as if there were nothing worse on earth than the disappearance of the moon. When B. then began to sweep the board, winning one song competition after another, and his portrait was to be added to Gallery of the Glorious, as we called them, at the music school, it took only one single institute party before you pulled the portrait off the wall with such force that the frame broke.

Sorry, you said, shrugging, and were already on your way to the bar for your next beer. The secretary of the institute called out: Artist! And immediately issued one of her house bans, which no one adhered to.

Don't irritate me, you once said. Then nothing will happen.

But that was not the problem. One time my neighbour stopped me, wanting to speak to me. She looked small and strange as she stood in front of me kneading her fingers next to the Monstera in the stairwell of the tenement house we had moved into. She was wearing a dress made of white lace, handed down from her grandmother, sewn from the best-quality peacetime goods, as the neighbour told me. Between her legs, the colour of her briefs shimmered through. She wore a dark leather belt and black Converses, with her hair up. Was the problem perhaps not in Voitto and me, but in this sick war waged in the back of our minds, which had already turned the words in our parents' mouths?

Why are you wearing my old nightdress? my neighbour's grandma had scolded her, and outside as well . . . For the love of . . . You will just get yourself noticed. But I want to get myself noticed, my neighbour had responded and shot her a laugh, as only our generation can laugh. And yet. The beautiful white dress now had a flaw in the fabric, since it now bore the disapproval of the one to whose trousseau it actually belonged. And because her grandmother had never talked about what it feels like to be chained to a barracks heater, she did not explain to her granddaughter on this occasion why one should avoid getting oneself noticed at any cost. But she understood all the same.

Last night, said the neighbour, kneading her fingers, there was something going on between you two again.

Us? I asked.

Should she, the neighbour wanted to know, have called the police?

Oh that, I said.

I see, right then, said the neighbour, trying not to look at my neck.

No, I said with complete conviction.

No, the neighbour repeated and smoothed her grand-mother's nightdress flat.

Monsters like us, you said once. But this time you said it in Finnish. I didn't understand and thought it was an endear-ment. You wrote it out on a piece of paper for me so that I could find it myself. It took a few days, but then I had worked it out.

You drove this Volvo 480, whose headlights you would raise and lower even if it wasn't dark at all. Can I borrow it? I asked.

If anything happens, I'll hold you responsible.

In the evening I called you. I had an accident, Voitto, I said for fun.

Don't you dare say you smashed it up.

I hung up and waited another moment. But why should you call back? After all, I had hung up. Then I went to rehearsal and thought of nothing but music.

It wasn't until the early evening that I got into the Volvo and drove off. In the curves I heard the chewing-gum papers slid-ing from side to side on the back shelf, along with a couple of broken cigarettes, a tuning fork, a Brainy Smurf figure and a crumbling piece of bog birch bark from Lapland that you had brought back from a visit home. I hadn't told anyone. The journey home took two hours.

During the journey I hummed the adagio of Beethoven's Sonata No. 14 in C minor to myself. You would have laughed at me! But since piano had been my second instrument, melodies went round in my head that would otherwise have been embarrassing. As if the black and white of the keys, the resonance of the strings in the wooden body of the instrument, the simultaneity of both clefs had set something in me free that I had believed well and truly closed off with the help of the violin. Something that was still there in the asthmatic wheezing of the harmonium, when Viktor operated the pedals underneath me with both hands and I sat high above him like an invincible ruler, with six fingers reaching in search of the music, as if no creature before me had ever played in a minor key. In the playing of the keys lived a monstrous golem, who vanquished anything that might cross your path. He was light and dark at the same time, he made me laugh and weep, a golem with respiratory problems that was not up to grappling with perfection. Monster enough to take on silence itself. Is it possible to weep like this when you hum a piece of which so many recordings have been made that its emotional impact should be that of a radio jingle? When I finished crying, the matter was settled. I stopped on the observation deck of the open-cast mine.

The sky stretched above this landscape of craters like a freshly washed tabletop. The rain poured quietly and without let up. No one was there but me. The flags of the Central German Lignite Company hung limp on the flagpoles and clanked in the wind like the masts of sailboats in the harbour of an artificial lake. Further ahead, just before the slope, there was a display board with all the destroyed villages marked, but I was too lazy to see if ours was there. I got up onto a picnic table that glinted with water, lit one of the two cigarettes, and looked down into the Grand Canyon of my childhood.

The absence of every landmark in the mining area was strange. Far below stood a shovel-wheel excavator, its steel wheel resting on the muddy ground. I found it surprisingly small until I noticed the tiny mobile excavators parked near it, like Viktor's Lego constructions on his nursery carpet. Those are moon probes, he once explained to me. I will reach the dark side of the moon in one of these. I will do it too, make no mistake.

Come to think, Viktor is the only person in my life that I fully and completely understand even when I don't understand him. I even understand him from a distance, even that of twenty-five years. You know, at that moment, standing on a picnic table on a Central German Lignite Company viewing platform, I suddenly found it perfectly logical that he always wanted to get as far away as possible. The rain ran down my face. Man, Viktor, I muttered into the half-light and closed my eyes. And he, ten or twenty years old, in that moment it didn't matter which, smiled his wrinkly smile.

When the cigarette got too wet to smoke, I drove on. I hadn't been back to the village for a long time. I had seen the removal of the church in Fly's film. Where was our house again? Oh yes, long gone. I sped through the streets that were still standing. In the dark windows of the 'Give Our Village a Future' Information and Advice Centre, I glimpsed the protest posters: *Our village lives. Still. The last one to leave should turn off the light. Let the Devil take the hindmost.* At the volunteer fire brigade I got out to lift the barrier. It had been a good summer for anything green. The front gardens in the cordoned-off area were wild and overgrown. At the gates of the old courtyards, the mallows had bolted. Grapes shone wet on the wild wines covering the walls. The pavement came to an end behind the old mill. I just kept going.

Apparently, the open-cast mine was being extended elsewhere at the moment. The slagheaps were sparsely covered with moss and grasses; in the last light of the day the tips of grass stalks glinted. I stopped on top of a hill. I turned off the engine, put on the handbrake and got out. Darkness had fallen, and I couldn't see how deep it was where it fell away in front of me. So, I got back into the car and stayed where I was. I couldn't think of anything better to do. For a while I watched the rain falling into the darkness ahead. Then I put my seat back and fell asleep.

The rain drummed down all night, interrupted by sporadic sounds of deer and foxes. In the middle of the night I was startled by deep noises that I couldn't identify. When I woke with a start and turned on the headlights, there was a wild boar right next to the passenger door, its narrow eyes reflecting the light. I quickly turned away so as to slip back into the darkness. I left the headlights on. At some point I lay down and dreamt that I was in my mother's belly. You'll come later, Dummy-doll, laughed Fly, It's my turn first. With my feet I pushed myself away from the soft reddish walls and had no sense of gravity.

The rain had stopped by morning. The Volvo stood on top of the last hill right in front of the gorge. A delicate autumn sky arched above it. I got out and squatted behind the boot to pee. Then I buttoned my trousers again, went round to the front, and reached into the car to release the handbrake. The second cigarette lay on the shelf; I took it out and smoked it in crackling gulps in the damp morning air. The birdsong from the oak forest further away could be heard even here. Finally, I placed my hands flat on the car bodywork and started to push.

As the Volvo began to pick up speed and roll towards the slope, I stopped. It rattled, a few stones flew up behind it, the earth began to slip. Then it was quiet. For a while I stood there, wet hands in my pockets. Then I turned round and left.

And here I am now. I'm still in the concert hall and I'm holding out against this applause, it's been going on for quite a while. And I think it's better not to keep looking for you. One last time I let my gaze pass over the rows in front of me, and suddenly in the tenth row I recognize Viktor's stocky figure. He laughs at me, and then raises two fingers of his right hand to make the peace sign. I think Viktor is the only one I don't have to tell this story to. He has grown older and even more wrinkled.

Then I turn and go to the piano. I check the seat height one last time. Everyone knows that Liszt is supposed not to have allowed his students to play Beethoven's *Moonlight* Sonata because he thought it too difficult. Gravity can be handled one way or another. Everything is there at the same time, past and present, that makes a difference. And we're still there too. So, there's no good reason not to dare to do it. I hope you hear this, Voitto. I'm starting now.

Fine